The
Fruit
Fell Far

The
Fruit
Fell Far

KRYS KING

theluvvsycalliance.com

Published by The LuvvSyc Alliance

ISBN: 978-0-9998228-6-9

Cover design and interior formatting:
Mark Thomas / coverness.com

Krystalynne King
Visit my website at www.KrysKing.com

Twitter.com/LuvvSyc

Instagram.com/LuvvSyc

Facebook.com/AuthorKrysKing

Either make the tree good and his fruit good,
Or else make the tree corrupt and his fruit corrupt;
For the tree is known by his fruit.
Matthew 12:33

Chapter One

"She is so strong."

"She is fake. You see her ass, what kind of first lady you know with an ass like that?"

"She is fine, huh?"

"Better be, paid all that money."

"She paid now for real."

"I heard they were having problems before this happened."

"I wish I could have been one of them problems, Pastor was fine!"

"I wonder if she will lead the Church now."

"Gavin Stone would be a good replacement."

"Why would she wear that lipstick with those shoes?"

"Why don't everybody just shut the hell up?!

Seriously. Damn." Simone had heard enough. She rolls her eyes at the crowd gathered by the bar that was only serving non-alcoholic beverages.

Simone throws back the rest of her iced tea that she had spiked with vodka and grimaces.

"Demons! All of you." Remarking at the pack, plopping her cup down on the nearby table and walks off; making her way toward where Kathy sat.

"I am so sorry for your loss Kat, if you need anything please let me know."

Simone approaches, bending down, and placing her hand on Kathryn's upper back. Kathryn says nothing in return, she just raises her head from where it rested in her lap and looked up at Simone as though she had the wrong person.

"What?" Kathryn asks, confused.

"Come. Kay, let's go lay down baby." Elizabeth advances, lifting her daughter up from the chair and leading her up the staircase to Kathryn's bedroom.

"Excuse us Simone honey. Thank you for coming."

"Of course, Mrs. Hill."

"I know this is hard Kay, but you'll get through this, the pain is only temporary. We can't have you reverting back to your old ways, you remember what happened last time?"

Elizabeth encourages her only child as they make their way into the sleeping quarters. Sitting her down on the bed, she begins to remove her shoes one at a time and push them under the bed.

"Did you see Betty-Maye? Didn't she look good? I can only imagine the heartbreak she must feel, losing her son so suddenly. I thought of Saul's concubine when I looked at her today. You know Rizpah watched her sons die? But when she was finally able to lay them to rest, she found peace. I wish that for the both of you. Give your sorrow to the Lord my dear." Beth continues to speak, laying Kathryn down on top of the bedspread, propping several pillows under her head.

Kathryn never acknowledges her mother or utters a word, she stares into space, eyes fixated on the ceiling.

"Get some rest sweetheart." Her mother states, kissing her on the forehead and exiting the room.

Kathryn continues to remain on the bed with her feet crossed at the ankle until she is sure the coast is clear and that her mom has made it back downstairs to attend to the vultures that called themselves the grieving family and friends but who will have their hands out tomorrow.

Once she is certain, she sits up and lets out a loud and long sigh that discharges all the air from her body. Picking up the pillows behind her, she starts to throw them onto the floor violently.

"Arghhhhh!" She yells out, getting up and walking into her bathroom. Gazing into the mirror she wipes away the smeared mascara from under her eyes and clears the lipstick that was outside the lines of her lips.

She opens the medicine cabinet and retrieves a pill bottle. Popping it open she pours a few of the oxycodone's she had prescribed from when she broke her foot last spring. Closing the container, she lays the pills down on the counter and uses the bottom of it to crush them into a powder. Leaning down she closes one nostril and snorts the chalky substance with the other.

The drugs go straight to her head, itching her nose. She rubs it intensely, trying to get the residue to go down. She rechecks her reflection to make sure there is no evidence present. Kathryn continues to stare at herself as she allows the feeling of ecstasy to cover her senses.

A wicked smile slowly creeps across her face as a male figure approaches her from behind and wraps his arms around her waist, landing his hands in between her thighs.

"How's my Kitty-Kat?" The deep voice asks into her ear with a whisper, resting his chin on her shoulder, making eye contact with her through the looking glass.

"Mmmmm." A moan escapes her mouth as she rests her head back onto his chest, granting him access to massage her clitoris, letting the high take over.

Moist, she turns to face him, enclosing her arms around his neck. Their lips touch and a tongue wrestles ensues.

"I need you." He states, breaking their kiss.

Kathryn puts her finger to his lips to halt any further words from coming out and says nothing. Lifting her bottom onto the bathroom sink, she hikes up her dress, revealing that there were no panties underneath.

Pulling him in, she begins to untuck his dress shirt and unbuckling the belt from around his slacks. The chocolate companion lets her have her way as he slips his hand under her dress and inserts his middle finger into her dripping slit.

"Ahhhh." Kathryn lets out, speeding up her undressing of him.

Pants undone and fallen to the floor, she whips out his dick and strokes it in an up and down motion, assuring that it is solid enough for insertion.

"Damn baby." He grunts, picking Kathryn up in his arms, holding her up and bringing her down onto him.

The sensation his rock-hard manhood gives to her insides causes her back to arch and she begins to move wildly, riding him as though it would be for the last time.

He tries to gain control by leaning her against the wall, grinding and quick stroking while his face is buried in her breast where he kisses, licks, and bites energetically.

Both at the point of climax the rhythm increases. The faster they move the harder they hit against the wall. The pictures and wall decor that were housed there begin to shake and clatter. The noise and the idea that someone may hear doesn't keep them from going full throttle.

"Shit!" The male yells out, exhausted and emptied.

The two fall to the marble tile, spent out.

"I love you Kitty." He reaches his hand over to place it in Kathryn's'.

His advance is not reciprocated, she snatches her hand away and stands, pulling down her dress and walking to the sink where she runs her finger across the counter, picking up any remnants of the pills and rubbing the findings on her gums. Sucking her finger, she walks back into the bedroom and drops back down on the bed, grabbing the remote from the nightstand and clicking on the television.

Her lover brings himself up from the floor and reapplies his clothing before following her.

"What the fuck is up yo?" His ego bruised. Awaiting an answer, he stands in the doorway, leaning against the frame buckling his belt.

"We need to stop what we're doing." She responds never looking away from the t.v.

Feeling his temperature start to rise and an uneasy feeling coming over him, he walks over to the bed and sits on the edge beside her. Slow-moving but deliberate he places his large left hand on her neck and constricts his fingers around it. Through clenched teeth he speaks, "Are you changing up on me bitch?"

Kathryn attempts to loosen his hold, but his grip is too tight.

"Huh?!" He asks, reinforcing his command, face stone cold.

There is a knock at the door.

8

Chapter Two

At the sound of the knock, they both look at the door, he gradually relaxes the muscles in his hand that still covered her neck. He pulls back and stands to his feet. Kathryn soothes her nape and turns on her side and focuses her attention back to the television screen, seeming unbothered.

There is a second knock and the door creeps open. Lucas; Kathryn's dad sticks in his head, "Everything okay baby girl?" He asks, opening the door fully and stepping inside.

"Well hey Lamar. How are you holding up?" Luke asks, acknowledging Lamar's presence and shaking his hand.

"Fine Mr. Hill, just fine. Just checking on my sister in-law, making sure she is okay. She is not really herself, ya know?" Lamar responds.

They both look over at the beautiful woman laying upon the bed spread, one who's eyes displayed sympathy and the other animosity.

Worry spreads across Lucas' face as his heart breaks for his little girl. He did not know what to do to make things better for his little butterfly, only time could take the pain away.

"Let's leave her be." He suggests, leading the way out the door.

Lamar Knight looks back at Kathryn and tries to burn a hole through her with his scowl, before closing the door behind him.

As the men make their way down the stairs, Lucas starts up conversation. "How's Ms. Betty doing?"

"The best that can be expected after losing your first born... Eric was the glue that held us together, it's going to be hard."

"It will be son, but we'll get through this together. We're still family, no matter what."

"Thank you, Mr. Hill, that means a lot."

"Enough with the Mister mess, didn't I just say we're family? Call me Luke." He states with a grin, patting him on the back. "Now let's go get some pie."

"How is she doing my love?" Beth comes up and crosses her arm in between her husbands' as they were making their way to the desert table.

"She's resting."

Tears that seemed uncontrollable, begin to fall from her eyes as thoughts of how her daughter must be feeling started to flood her head. She pulls her spouse closer and lays her head on his arm and closes her eyes, unknowingly keeping him from the pecan pie he had been eyeing since the repass started.

Lucas forgets about the pie that was down to its last two slices and gives his wife what she needs at that moment. He kisses the top her head and uses his available arm to throw around her and hold her tight.

"Hello Mr. and Mrs. Hill. Hi Lamar." Stephanie McDaniel stands in front of the trio with a distressed expression on her face and a cup clenched between her hands.

"Hi Steph." Everyone responds. Elizabeth unleashing Lucas and embracing Stephanie in a hug.

"I just wanted you guys to let Kathy know not to worry about the anything. I will handle the day to day things at the church until she is ready to return."

"Thank you darling. I don't know what Kat would do without you." Beth replies briefly running her palm across the side Stephanie's face.

"It's no problem. Give her my best." Stephanie remarks, shooting a smile, placing down her drink and exiting the Knight estate.

Lamar and the Hills stand in silence as they look at all the people who came out to give their condolences and celebrate the person the city of Atlanta considered to be the man that uplifted the people and who strived to improve the lives of the entire community through God's promise.

"I'm going to start to put the food away." Elizabeth says to Lucas, leaning in for a quick kiss.

"Okay sweetheart. Hopefully people will begin to realize it's time to go home. Kat could use the peace and quiet." Luke responds. "Save me a piece of Ella's pie."

Chapter Three

The 20,000-square foot home was cold and dark when Kathryn emerged from her bedroom, but she was glad she had convinced her parents that she would be fine alone.

Walking into her office that was adjacent to where she slept, she sits at her desk and powers on the computer. While it wakes up she scoots her chair back and stands to briefly run to the kitchen.

She grabs a glass from the wine rack and pulls out a bottle of Cabernet from the fridge. Pulling the cork out with her teeth she fills the glass to the rim and sips from the crystal, returning to her PC with cup and bottle in tow.

Placing the glass and bottle down, her eye catches a picture of her and Eric, showing them in their early days of dating, he had taken her hiking at Drayton Park, she had remembered it as one of the happiest times in her life and the trail had become one of her favorite places to hike as well as a source of solace. Her face twists and frowns at the memory, she slams the photo down onto the desktop, so it is no longer looking back at her; breaking the frame. She pulls a cigarette case from the desk drawer, opening it and pulling out one of the tightly rolled joints and lighting it.

If her parents and the members of Alpha and Omega could see her now. She was no longer the person she had been pretending to be for so long. She was no longer the first lady that her following deserved or the God-fearing woman her parents had raised. She was an empty vessel now. Kathryn didn't know if there was a point in time that things changed or if she had been this person all along.

Taking a long drag she signs into her Apple computer and clicks around hastily until her mission was complete.

She reclines back in her chair and brings her feet up onto the desk and takes another pull from her joint, contemplating.

Mulling over Lamar and the attitude he displayed earlier had her irked. He was only supposed to be a quick and good fuck, nothing more, but now he was on some more shit.

Tilting forward she picks up her glass and brings it to her lips and tips it into her mouth, falling back against the seat once again. She closes her eyes and fails at the attempt to clear her mind of all thoughts and recollections of days gone by.

She had decided to leave early from Heaven's Healing; Kathryn's foundation for helping families and individuals who have been through traumatic events, she opts to head home and get an early start on dinner before Eric returned from his counseling session at the Church. Stopping by Edgar's Grocery on the way, she called Eric to see if there was anything that he needed while she was out.

He didn't answer the phone, so she just picked up a couple things that she knew he liked and checked out.

Mary J.'s 25/8 was in the midst of playing on Jams 95.4 when Kat cranks up the car. She loved that song and it depicted everything she was feeling up to that point in her life. An idea popped into her head at that moment and she decides to give Eric another call, this time leaving a message when the voicemail came on.

Hi Baby. Just wanted to tell you how much I love you and how blessed I feel to have such a wonderful man in my life. I have a surprise for you when you get home. See you tonight.

Using the button on the steering wheel she ends the call and message, she cranks the volume, pops on her shades, and makes her way home.

Pulling up to the house she and Eric shared, she decided that since she only had a few bags, she would park in the driveway instead of the garage.

Stepping out and grabbing the groceries with one hand, still singing Mary's song out loud, she walks up to the entry, unlocks the door, and proceeds inward.

That's odd. Kathryn had said to herself when she notices the alarm system didn't go off. She shrugs it off, assuming either her or Eric had forgotten to arm it when leaving out that morning.

Stepping inside the kitchen, she places the bags down on the counter, going over to open the refrigerator to begin the restock.

Grabbing the milk and butter from one of the

bags, she turns to go place them in their appropriate compartment when she hears something coming from the end of the hall. Stopping in her tracks, she freezes to see if she hears it again.

What was that? She asked herself. Quietly placing the produce down in front of her, she tip-toes in the direction of the sound, picking out a knife from the holder on the way. The noise was coming from the bedroom; her heart begins to pace rapidly.

The door was halfway open. Kathryn approaches snakingly, propping against the wall to make sure she wasn't spotted. Angling her head forward to peek in, the breath is knocked out of her as though she had just been punched in the stomach.

Eric sat at the front on the bed, naked, legs spread shoulder width apart, and feet planted firmly on the floor. Simone Clark was on her knees in between his legs, sucking slowly but sloppily on his manhood. Eric sits back, resting on his arms, head hung downward, eyes closed, appearing to be in bliss as he moans and licks his lips. He brings a hand to her head to guide her movement, which causes her to turn up the speed. She begins running the hand opposite the one stroking him up his chest, she pinches his nipples with her fingers.

Kathryn jerks her head back against the wall and struggles to fill her lungs with air. Tears begin to fall as she realizes what is going on. Everything in her told her to go in there and start whooping ass but something else came over her, a feeling all too familiar. The tears stopped, and her breathing leveled. She exhaled deeply and wiped her face to rid any trace of waterworks.

Kat looks back one more time to make sure she saw what she saw; once confirmed she made her way back into the kitchen and continued to put up the items she had just purchased.

After the groceries where put away, Kathryn sneaks out of her house and drives away as though she was never there.

Kathy brings her feet down from the desk and takes one last pull of the marijuana and puts it out on the picture frame she had just shattered. She rises from her seat, grabs her half full glass and refills it, and moves for the bathroom. She was fixed on taking a shower and getting todays funk off her; however, although she hoped it would, the heat and steam from the water does not stop her mind from drifting back into the past. She places her hands up on the shower wall and bends her head down under the shower head, letting the stream fall over her.

That day Kat went along with things as normal after witnessing the adultery. She didn't understand how her husband could break the vow he made to her and to God. Questions of why and how long embedded themselves in the front of her brain, screaming out to be answered every five seconds.

This is all a test, it had to be, the Lord never puts more on us than we can bare. He wants to make sure that we are in this no matter what obstacles may come our way.

She told herself.

She had come home at the time she always had, prepared dinner, and had it waiting on him when he returned home.

"K? Honey, I'm home." He had said as though things were business as usual. He had placed his briefcase and keys down on the table in the foyer per his routine and made his way to where the smells where coming from.

Kathryn was at the stove putting the finishing

touches on her tomato sauce. Eric comes up behind her and wraps his arms around her waist, kissing her nape softly. Kat's skin crawls. Not only because no matter what the circumstance, his touch always sent chills down her spine, but today that feeling included disgust. How could he come home and hug all up on her like he wasn't just screwing the Director of Youth Activities.

"Hi, are you hungry?" She greeted nonchalantly, patting his hands, indicating that he needed to move so she could remove the pot from the heat.

"Of course, I'm always in the mood for your famous spaghetti sauce." He replies, unbuttoning his blazer and walking over to the dining room table. He takes his designated seat at one end of the 8-seater table, throwing his coat on the back of the chair.

The table is already set with wine and silverware. Eric helps himself to a glass as Kathryn made her way over with two dinner plates. She places one down in front of him and takes her seat at the opposite end of the table. They both simultaneously pull their napkins from the table and lay them in their lap.

Without prompting, Eric began to say grace.

"Amen." They both said once the prayer was completed.

"This looks great Kat." Eric complimented his wife, reaching for his fork.

Kathryn grins slightly trying to control her emotions.

"How was your day sweetheart?" He goes on to ask.

"How long Eric?" Kathryn asked, bringing her eyes up from her plate and up to those of her husband, unable to fake it.

"How long what honey?"

Kathy lifts her hands, clasps them together in front of her and rests her chin atop them and exhales.

"How long have you been having an affair?"

Chapter Four

Kathryn turns the water off, opens the shower door, steps out, and grabs a towel from the shelf to her right. Drying off she is frustrated at the feelings overcoming her, she shakes her head forcefully trying to stop herself from delving back into the past. Picking up her wine from the sink, she gulps it down without pause. Depleted, she refills the glass, emptying the last of the alcohol into it.

Feeling like walking around in her natural form, she does not dress, but instead, walks unadorned into the bedroom and sits at her vanity, where she applies cream to her body. She catches her image in the mirror and is greeted with flashes of even more scenes she thought she had long forgotten.

Eric had thrown his fork down on the table, picking

up the napkin, wiping his mouth and throwing it down as well.

"Kat what are you talking about? Where is this coming from?"

"Let's not play games Eric? You should know better than anyone that what we do in the dark will always come to light."

Tears began to fall from Kathryn's eyes, she quickly wipes them away. Eric removes himself from his seat and walks over to where she sat. Kathryn's beauty was something that Eric always found himself appreciating, even then, when she was clearly upset, all he saw was her voluminous caramel body covered perfectly in the Donna Karen dress he bought her a few months backs. He wanted to get close enough to touch her, to feel the warmth of her skin against his. The tears that were falling from her almond shaped hazel eyes made her face glistened and turned him on even more at that moment. He places his hands on to hers, and she quickly snatches them away. She jumps up from the table and walks over to the other side of the room.

"Stop playing with me! I know! I know about you and

Simone, now how long as it been going on?"

She turned to her husband to receive his response, face wet with sadness, anger, and pain. She is greeted with a hardened face, Eric's jaw clenched, and eyes squinted. He wasn't in the mood for her self-righteousness. He despised being criticized and called out on what he was or wasn't doing. In his mind, if the bills were being paid, he wasn't bringing home any illegitimate children, and he made sure she didn't want for anything, he was doing his part.

"So, what are you going to do? Leave me? Huh?" He asked standing. "You going to leave me and destroy everything I've built, lose all of this?" He states with a daring tone waving his arms around and landing them on the table, leaning in, exuding intimidation.

Kathryn could not believe his reaction, she figured he would fall to her feet and beg for forgiveness, like King David.

"I have been called to minister God's word, to get his children into his house, through his gates. If one of the members need a little attention and affection to get them there, then I must do what I must. Do you understand that 'K'?"

"What?" Is all she could get out.

Eric straightens his stance and slowly walks over to her, sticking his hands in his pants pocket. "Kat, Simone means nothing to me." He removes his hands and attempts to grab hers again.

"I am your wife Eric! How could you?!" She yells, dumbfounded at the way he was talking.

He approaches her again, gently bringing his palm up to her face, gazing into her eyes. "I love you."

"You should leave." She slaps his hand away."

"What?"

"Leave!"

"Kathryn."

"Leave! Leave now Eric!"

Kathryn shakes herself out of the trance she had fallen into. She rubs cream in between her hands and fingers, exhausted from the flood of memories that ran through her head. She looks at her reflection in the mirror and doesn't recognize the person staring back at her, so much has happened in the last few months, and now her husband was gone.

Eric didn't put up much of a fight that night after being told to get out. He quietly walked over, picked up his keys and briefcase to exit the home. She had followed him screaming and shouting, picking up a glass vase and throwing it at him, missing, it clashes against the door as he shut it behind him.

Kathryn falls to the floor and let the pain she had been trying to imprison since she witnessed her husband's infidelity escape her. She is startled at the sudden ringing of the residence phone. Inhaling her sobs, she sits frozen, not sure what to do. She lets the answering machine pick up. It was her mother.

"Katty, it's mom. I was just checking in, give me a…"

"Hello." Kathryn picks up the phone and speaks in between sniffles. She wasn't sure why she answered, she honestly hated talking to her mother, but she also loved her very much and needed her at that moment.

"Oh Katty, you're home. How are you sweetheart?"

"Fine."

"You don't sound fine, is everything okay?"

"It's nothing. Eric and I just had a fight."

"Well, no one said marriage would be easy. I'm sure it isn't the first and it won't be the last."

"I put him out." Kathryn responds dryly, her tears ceasing to fall and her demeanor hardening. She

26

detested when her mom talked as though she knew it all.

"Now why would you go and do something like that?" Elizabeth asks, sitting up in her bed, removing her reading glasses, nudging a sleeping Luke beside her.

"Because he's cheating on me that's why!" Kathryn's voice elevates.

"Oh Katty, I'm sorry." There is silence. "Listen sweetheart, men will be men. Eric loves you, and remember through good and bad, through thickness and thin, till death, that is the vowel you took. The Lord will never put you or your marriage through anything that he didn't believe you could come back from."

"Good-bye mother." She wasn't in the mood.

"Katty, wait."

Click

Chapter Five

Turning the top and closing the body cream, Kathryn picks up her wine glass she stands, walking over to the entertainment center where she turns on some music. Forgetting the last CD, she had listened to was the greatest hits from Dorothy Moore; her sultry vocals on "Misty Blue" fills her ears.

She begins to sway back and forth to the music, and cranks the volume to where it fills up the entire second floor. Picking up her joint and relighting it, she is immediately transported back to the past.

Hey Kitty-Kat." Kathryn is addressed by Lamar as she lays in the back lawn by the pool.

She lifts her shades up onto her forehead to get a look at the person who just spoke to her. "What I tell you about calling me that Lamar?" She replied, letting her sunglasses fall back over her eyes.

"You know you like it." He had said with a laugh, sitting down on one of the lounge chairs beside her. Kat says nothing in return.

"Where is Eric?" He changes the subject.

"Who cares." Was the only response he received. Kathryn did not watch her words when it came to Lamar Knight. He wasn't anybody in her eyes. He was a 36-year-old man that was still living at home with him mom, and who's only job consisted of nickel and diming to the neighborhood school kids. Lamar was the black sheep of the family for sure.

"Well damn Sis, it's like that." Lamar reacts, picking up Kathy's cocktail and drinking from it.

"What the hell do you want Lamar?" Kathy's asks annoyed. She was finding it more and more difficult to hold her tongue. Eric had come back home a few weeks prior and they hadn't said more than two words to each other. They put up a façade for the church and community but behind closed doors, the temperature was below zero.

"I just came to holla at you guys for a while, that's all. You sure do have a nasty mouth to be a woman of

God, you know that?"

Kathryn, took off her shades, placed them down on the patio table and turns to look at Lamar. To be a bum he was a fine one. Tall chiseled dark chocolate, low cut, shaped up mustache and goatee; which framed his smooth plump lips, covering his pearly white teeth. Having not been touched intimately by a man in a while, and her mind in a state to where she was taking in everything around her, Lamar was looking mighty good to her, sitting there glistening in the heat of the sun.

"What?" Lamar asks noticing the way he was being looked at. He had always found Kat to be the most beautiful woman he had ever seen, and she gave him yet another reason to be jealous of his older brother. He had looked at her with lust filled eyes on many occasions and now it appeared that she was looking back at him in that same way.

"Nothing." Kathy states, turning back on her back, looking out onto the infinity pool and the city view.

Lamar got up from where he was sitting and went over and sat at the edge of Kathryn's chair, placing a hand on her thigh. "Are you happy?"

"I am the happiest I have ever been." Kat responds glaring at Lamar, no feeling in her voice. She is uncomfortable with him being that close, but at the same time, weirdly turned on, and she knew he knew she was not being truthful.

She allows his hand to stay where he had laid it, and he slowly slides his hand up and down her leg, never breaking eye contact.

"You know I am here for you if you ever need me, right? For anything." He lets her know guiding his hand in between her thighs and moving upward toward her box.

Kat fidgets in her seat. "Lamar what are you doing?"

Although she said the words she doesn't stop Lamar's advances, and he doesn't waste this moment, he proceeds to do everything he had dreamed of before she changed her mind.

He caresses her pussy through her swimsuit bottom and she let out a sound of pleasure. Lamar stands and falls to his knees where he pushed her bikini panties to the side, exposing her Brazilian wax. Taking in all her glory, he pulls her by her legs, bringing her closer to him and her wet kat closer to his face.

He applies smalls pecks down on her clitoris, and when she lets out a wail he dives in sucking and licking, eating her until she came, sopping up all her juices not letting one drop fall.

Kathryn lays there unable to move, partially because of the feeling of ecstasy covering her body, but mostly because she couldn't believe what just happened. She stares up at the umbrella that was perched above, shielding her from the sun. Lamar brings himself up and sits beside her. Wiping his mouth, he comes in to kiss her.

"No. Don't."

Lamar halts. "What?"

"Just don't." Kathryn sits up and fixes her swimsuit. She looks up at Lamar and into his eyes, and says nothing.

They hold each other's glare for what seemed like a lifetime. Lamar, looking to see if they would be doing it again, and Kathryn wishing her husband still looked at her the way his brother did. Kathryn breaks the stare, grabs her cocktail and stands to go inside.

"Where you going?" Lamar calls after her. The

smile of intrigue quickly leaves his face and one of disappointment appears as he notices Eric walking through the double doors onto the patio. He leans back on the chair, seeing that Kathryn didn't acknowledge her husband's presence but continues to walk by him without speaking.

"Kathy." Eric greets his wife, extending his arm, attempting to stop her stride. When she keeps walking past him without at least looking in his direction, he turns his attention back in front of him, continuing to make his way to where his brother sat.

Chapter Six

The sound of the CD skipping brings Kathryn back to the present. She had had enough of the flashbacks and she was beyond buzzed. Glancing over at the clock sitting on the nightstand she notices it is going on 6AM. Kathryn decides that she is not going to try to sleep, but instead that she is going to go down the street to Charlette's café. They should be opening any minute and she could really use one of their lattes and a hot egg and spinach breakfast sandwich.

Throwing on some clothes, Kathryn heads out the front door, oblivious to the fact that she is being followed.

Starting the engine and reversing out of the driveway, the lurker waits until she is a little way down the road before cranking up, turning on his lights, and pulling out behind her.

Charlette's Café was a cozy quaint coffee and tea bar in Peachtree Corners that Kathryn found herself at least three times a week.

Sun beginning to rise, she is right on time as she sees Charise, one of the owners inside flicking on the lights and taking chairs from on top of the tables.

"Good Morning." Kathy is greeted by Charise.

"Morning Charise."

"It's a bit early for you, don't you think?" Charise showed concern, knowing that her first lady had just buried her husband less than twenty-four hours earlier.

Kathy was not in the mood for anyone's sympathy or their opinion on how she should be handling her husband's passing. "Just need a coffee and something to eat before heading over to the church."

"Sure thing. Have a seat, I'll have your usual ready in a sec."

Coffee in hand, Kathy takes off toward the exit, making her way to her car.

As she looks at the meter to make sure she was in good time, her attention is grabbed by a flashing of light in the distance.

Her pursuer who sat in his dark sedan ducked off in the shadows, quickly throws his camera down in the passenger seat and slowly inches down in the drivers, hoping he wasn't spotted.

Kathryn shrugs it off and proceeds to getting into her car. Seeing that his quarry was still unaware of his position, he straightens his posture and puts his car into drive, curious of their next destination.

Chapter Seven

Kathryn pulls up to Alpha & Omega Church of Worship and parks in her designated parking space. She notices a car in her rear-view mirror turning into the parking lot and backing into one of the many vacant spaces. Katy found this to be strange, seeing that her car was the only other car out there but they chose to park a good football field from the entrance.

Noting the car into her memory bank she turns her attention back to the task at hand, and steps out and makes her way into the sanctuary.

Walking into the church heat begins to rise up from her toes and sweat trickles down her brow. A heavy sigh escapes her mouth and she pushes forward through the halls and into her office.

"What do you think you are doing?"

"Kathryn!"

Maurice McNeal, the church treasurer was caught read handed. Kathryn turned on the light to her office to find Maurice searching frantically through her desk in the dark.

"What are you looking for in the dark Maurice?"

"Its not that dark First Lady. Just figured why turn on the lights when the sun is shining through." He answers pointing to the window on the left side of the room.

"Mmm Hmm." Kathryn wasn't buying it. For one, it was cloudy out due to the impending rain, so the sun was nowhere to be found.

Maurice could tell she wasn't falling for it. He wipes his palms that were damp with perspiration on his legs. "I was just looking for the quarterly statements for Internal Revenue, it's about time I get them over to them."

Kathryn starts walking over to her desk. "Now Maurice you know I don't have those documents."

"Well I thought…"

Kathryn throws her hand up in the air cutting him off. She places her purse atop her desk. "No, you didn't but whatever, please get out Maurice."

Delighted at the idea, Maurice doesn't hesitate to remove himself.

Kathryn knew Maurice wasn't being truthful. She looks around her office to see if anything was missing when there was a knock at her door.

"Not now Maurice." She starts before looking up. There is a man there, but it is not Maurice. "I'm sorry, can I help you?"

He wasn't expecting her to be so stunning. The picture he had in his folder did her no justice. Kathryn Hill-Knight stood before him, no taller than 5 feet four in a navy-blue dress that fit her form with perfection. Her flawless skin glowed in the dim lighting. It was as though she had no clue just how gorgeous she was, which made her disarming and intriguing.

"Listen, I hate to be short, but if you can come back in a few hours, there will be someone out front that can assist you."

He shakes off whatever had come over him. "I'm sorry. Excuse me." He smooths is tie and clears his throat. "I'm Keith Crane, a detective with the Atlanta Police Department." He flashes his badge. "I just needed to as you a few questions."

"I don't know what I could possibly do for you detective, my husband is dead. He died of a brain aneurysm. I'm sure you know that we buried him yesterday."

"I'm afraid its not that easy Mrs. Knight, there has been some developments.

Kathryn comes around to the front of her desk and sits on the edge of it.

"What kind of developments?" She crosses her arms and a look of confusion comes across her face.

"Murder."

Chapter Eight

"Murder? What do you mean murder?" Kathryn stands and steps forward toward the detective.

Crane is taken aback at her sudden advancement towards him. He takes a slight step backwards but takes the chance to get a better look at her. It takes everything he has inside him, to not to drown in her deep brown eyes that were shaped like little canoes and full of mystery.

"Detective?" Kathy prods, after she receives no response to her inquiry.

"Turns out your husband may not have died from complications in the brain, but was killed."

"You have to be joking right?"

"I'm afraid I'm not Mrs. Knight." Detective Crane takes a seat and pulls out a notepad and pen from his blazer pocket. "Now can you tell me the events that occurred the day of August 11?"

Kathryn takes the seat neighboring to where Crane sat. "Well it was a day like any other Sunday."

Kathy fixates her eyes onto a portrait of her and Eric and allows her mind to drift as she recalls the day her husband died right before her eyes.

"Now we've all heard the saying, what's done in the dark will always come to the light. And that's the truth! Everything that is done outside of God's will, isn't nothing but darkness. Drugs, alcohol, fornication, adultery; all darkness. Have we forgotten that the All Mighty sees everything? If we can't keep our secrets from those around us, how can we expect the Lord not to know? But thank God for his grace!"

"Glory!" I jump up and praise as I listen to the word come out of my husband's mouth. He was the pastor at Alpha and Omega Church of Worship and I was the First Lady of this 325,000 square-foot church.

"Now, Kathryn and I will open the doors of the church." He walked up to me and grabs my hand, leading me to the middle of the stage. Malcolm, our sound technician walks over, and hands me a microphone.

"Now how about that sermon?!" I yell out to the audience. "God spoke straight through Pastor today; can I get an Amen?" The congregation that was filled with family, friends, believers, and serpents, roared to their feet in applause, praise, and joy. Eric who still held my hand, bought it up to his lips to kiss. As I smile at him and make eye contact I see that his eyes begin to roll to the back of his head. The joyous expression that was upon my face quickly turns into that of fright. Before I could ask are you alright, he falls to the floor and begins to seize. I fall to the floor beside him.

"Someone call 911!" I yelled in hysterics. Next thing you know, I'm in an ambulance on my way to the hospital.

Kathryn's eyes began to swell, and she could feel and outburst coming on at the flashback. She takes her focus off the painting and drags them over to meet with those of the detective, tears quietly streaming down her face. Crane is overwhelmed with compassion. He comes over to where she sat and props up on the arm of the chair, wrapping an arm around her shoulder.

"I just can't believe he's gone." She weeps, leaning

her head down in his lap.

Uneasy, Detective Crane winces, picking her head up before she felt the rise in his jeans. "Can you think of anyone that may have wanted to hurt Pastor Knight?"

Kathryn brings up her head and wipes her nose. "Well yes and no. Eric was a wonderful man, devoted to his community." She drops her hands into her lap.

"But?" Crane insist that she continues.

"But in getting where he was, he crossed a lot of people."

"Can you provide me with any names?" The Detective places the pan against the paper anticipating her answer.

"Well I don't know. I guess I will have to start with Maurice McNeil. I caught him in here snooping before you arrive. Are you for certain Eric was murdered?"

"We are. Appears to be poisoning."

Chapter Nine

"First Lady?" Stephanie was not only surprised to see Kathryn at the church, but she also wasn't expecting to see her in the middle of an intimate exchange with a male stranger.

Crane and Kathryn were startled by the abrupt intrusion. They both look toward the door, finding Stephanie, the church secretary standing there beneath the threshold, with folders in her arms.

"Stephanie, hi." Kathryn rises to her feet, while quickly swiping at the tears that were perched on her cheeks. "This is Detective Crane with Atlanta PD. He just came to ask some follow up questions."

"Good Morning."

"Morning Detective." Stephanie returns the greeting, a little perturbed at an officer being there and the first lady's obvious distressed appearance.

"Thank you for stopping by Detective, I wish I could be of more help."

"I think you can."

"Excuse me?"

Crane notices the defense in Kathryn's tone. "I just mean you can by allowing me to take a walk around the premises, ask a few questions that's all."

Kathryn, clearing her throat, "Of course. Stephanie, do you mind showing Detective Crane around?"

"Absolutely not First Lady. Right this way Detective."

Stephanie escorts Crane out and into the hallway. As soon as they are out of sight Kathryn rapidly saunters over to her desk, procures her belongings, and departs through the back of the church, hoping to avoid anyone else that chose to show up today.

She jumps in her silver Mercedes Benz S-Class coupe and slams the door shut behind her.

Kathryn screams out in horror at the knock on her driver side window.

It was Lamar.

"Open the door!"

"What do you want?" She asks without rolling down

the window or opening the door as instructed.

"Open the door Kathy!"

Kathryn opens the door reluctantly.

"Scoot over." Lamar orders, pushing her, letting her know that he was going to be driving.

"What are you doing Lamar?"

"We need to talk."

"You couldn't have just called?"

"Would you have answered?" Lamar looks over to Kathryn who is now in the passenger seat, daring her to say yes.

She doesn't answer his question but asks one of her own. "Where are we going?"

"Just sit back and relax. It's a surprise."

Kathryn sits silently as Lamar steers her vehicle out onto the street. When she sees that he is signaling to turn onto the highway, she opens her mouth.

"How did you know where I was? Have you been following me?"

"I knew you could only be one or two places, home or church." Lamar answers, eyes glued to the road and both hands on the wheel.

"Where are you taking me Lamar?"

"Somewhere we can be alone."

"We are alone." She gets no reaction. "Lamar!" Silence. "You're scaring me!"

This catches his attention. Lamar takes his right hand from the swivel and places it on Kathryn's left thigh. "I would never hurt my Kitty Kat, you know that."

Kathryn tries to move closer to the passenger door to make herself harder to reach but Lamar has a long wing span. "Would you hurt Eric?" She asks in a low mumble, looking down at his hand clenching her leg.

"What?" Her question takes Lamar by surprise. He finally takes his eyes off the road and faces her, wanting to know what she was talking about.

"Eric was murdered.

Chapter Ten

Kathryn's head jerks forward as Lamar slams on the breaks. As he pulls over onto the shoulder, cars behind them blow their horns and scream obscenities out their windows.

"What the fuck did you just say?" He throws the car in park and turns completely in the seat to where he is facing her.

"Eric was murdered?" Kathryn reiterates, rubbing her neck.

What the fuck you mean murdered? Don't play with me Kit."

"A detective was at the church and he said Eric died because someone wanted him that way. Poisoning." She looked up at him not only to see what his response would be to the news, but also to see the expression on his face when he reacted to it.

"And you thought I had something to do with it?"

"Well." Is all she says, shrugging her shoulders.

"Ain't you the one who was running to the car like you stole something."

"I was shaken up."

"Yeah or feeling guilty."

"You know what? Fuck you Lamar!"

"Fuck me, huh?" The look Kathryn was learning all too well came across Lamar's face, and she knew she has pushed a button. She sees his hand coming for her throat once again when she notices something out the corner of her eye.

"Lamar!" She yells out and points to the window.

"What?" Lamar looks to see what or who had Kathy startled.

"That car. I think it has been following me. I seen it leaving the house, at the café, then at the church, and now there it is again."

As she filled Lamar in, the black sedan with tinted out windows and out of state tags slowly went passed them on the roadway, getting off on the next exit. "You sure that's the same car?"

"Lamar, I'm sure. Do you know who that is?"

"What in the hell makes you think I know who it is?" Lamar glances over at Kathryn and he can tell that she is really frightened. The shit had his interest peaked as well. First, they get news that his brother didn't just die but was killed and now they were being followed. He reaches down to his leg and pulls up a 9-millimeter that was strapped to it, cocks it to load one in the chamber, then rests it on his lap.

"Why do you have a gun?" Fear and shock expresses itself on her face. "What are you going to do Lamar?"

He doesn't acknowledge her inquiry, instead he shifts the gears into drive and pulls back onto the freeway full speed to the Roswell exit where he gets off with a goal of finding the motorist.

It was like he knew exactly where to go, after making the right off the exit, they spot the car at the Exxon.

Lamar pulls Kathryn's car around the back of the convenient store and brings it to a stop.

"Lamar?"

"Stay here." He demanded.

Lamar jumps out the car, pistol in hand, and walks up on the back of the building. Just as he was approaching, a man emerges from the men's room.

Lamar pushes the man against the dumpster outside the restroom and points his gun at his head.

"Who are you? Why are you following us?" Kathryn heard Lamar ask. She could tell his question was being answered but had a difficult time hearing what the stranger had to say. Apparently, it was something Lamar didn't like because he punches the guy in the stomach violently, causing him to plummet to the ground and Kathryn to cover her ears to obscure the painful moans that escapes the sufferer.

"Hey, what is going on out there?" A loud Indian accent cuts through the noise.

Kathryn peeps through a squinted eye, seeing Lamar running toward her car. He jumps in, not saying a word, pulling off, and simultaneously flinging his gun under the seat.

"Who was that? Are you okay?" Kathryn wanted to know if he found out anything. The only reaction she received was him wiping the moisture from his forehead then cutting up the volume on the stereo, drowning out her questioning.

"What did he say? What just happened?" She yells

THE FRUIT FELL FAR

over the loud rhyming of Lil' Wayne.

"Not right now, I need to think."

"You need to think?! What do you need to think about?"

Lamar doesn't say another word. He maximizes the volume and remains intensely engrossed on the road before him.

Chapter Eleven

They ride in silence until he pulls into a driveway at a house Kathryn had never seen before.

"Where are we?"

"My crib."

"What? Since when?"

"Almost a month."

Kathryn was astonished. Lamar was finally out of his mother's house. The one-story brick ranch style residence wasn't as nice as the one and her and Eric had shared, but it fit him.

Lamar picks up his gun from under the seat and straps it back to his leg and gets out. Kathryn is right behind him, looking around as she walked, checking her surroundings. Once inside, Lamar marches over to the sofa and conceals his weapon under one of the cushions.

"This is nice Lamar." Kathryn compliments the way he had the place put together.

"Thank you. I got it for us."

"For us?" His statement had thrown her for a loop.

"Yeah, but fuck that shit right now though Kitty. Sit down." Lamar points down at the couch.

Kathryn could tell that he and the situation was serious, so she does as she was instructed. Lamar hovers over her, glaring at her with an expressionless face for what seemed like an eternity before he sat down on the coffee table in front of her.

"What is it?" She questions, returning his gaze.

"Frank West."

"Huh?"

"Dude back at the store. His name is Frank West."

"Okay, who is that? And why has he been following me?"

"He's the younger brother of Adam West."

"Adam? From college?"

"How many nigga's you know named Adam West Kit?"

"This makes no sense. Why didn't he just speak?

What did he say? Is he okay? You didn't hurt him too bad, did you?" Lamar is bombarded with questions, but he never flinches, and his countenance remains the same.

"How do you know him?"

"I don't. I mean, Adam and I dated for a few months back in college, but I've never met any of his family." Perplexed, she rubs her hand on her temple.

"Adam committed suicide shortly before I moved down south."

"That's the thing, this man don't think it was suicide. Says his brother would never do anything like that. Homie think you know more than you were letting on."

"What?! That's ridiculous." Kathryn leaps to her feet, lingering over Lamar with disbelief in her eyes, shocked that he could even come to her with something like that.

"Now look Kitty, I love you. Since the day I met you, I've loved you. Keep it real with me, what happened?" Lamar stands to face her, laying his hands on her shoulders, looking into her eyes. Kathryn swipes his arms out her way and walks from him to the fireplace where she sees a picture of her and Lamar sitting on the mantle. It was taken by Eric and Lamar's mom at a cookout last year. She picks up the picture, scrutinizing it.

"Lamar this is crazy. He is mistaken or high, one or the other. Did you get his information? I need to speak with him."

"Buddy gave his card." He pulls it from his back pocket, but hesitates to give it to her. "He seemed pretty convinced. You know I got your back no matter what, but I can't help you if you don't be honest with me."

Studying him, Kathryn could tell he had been persuaded and that he was genuinely worried.

Lamar was so different from Eric. Kathryn believed that to be the reason she was attracted to him. He had a soft and loving side, but his rough bad boy side did something to her.

"Lamar, sweetie, I promise this is one big misunderstanding. Let's sit."

She gently pushes him down on the sofa with one hand and pulling the card from his fingers with the other. Climbing in his lap, she rests a leg on either side of him. Welcoming her, her rests his hands on her hips.

"I love you too Lamar." She lightly kisses his lips.

"Yeah?"

"Yea baby."

They kiss passionately, wrestling their tongues.

BANG!

Kathryn's ears ring at the loud blast.

During their make out session she had snakingly reached beneath the couch cushions and retrieved Lamar's firearm, held it to the side of his head and pulled the trigger without a second thought.

Chapter Twelve

Kathryn

"Got-damnit!" I yell out. This is some shit for real.

Throwing the gun down beside Lamar, my eyes become paralyzed, stuck on his body, that was surely getting colder by the minute. Adrenaline begins to pump through my veins with the quickness, I start to pace back and forth. I had to think this through.

Lamar had obviously just killed himself, guilt-ridden from killing his only brother out of jealousy. That's what I will say to anyone who asked.

This is not supposed to be happening. I should have handled me being followed on my own, but Crane showing up threw me off, had me paranoid. I just didn't understand that piece.

I walk into the kitchen to fix a glass of water, trying to calm down, so I can think clearly. My heart is in my chest and my hands are shaking violently.

Sipping the water from the glass, I realize I'm leaving genetic material all over the place. I instantly pour the water down the drain and grab a paper towel and wipe it dry, removing my fingerprints.

I put the glass back where I took it, rip off a few more napkins, and retrace my steps, clearing any sign that I had been there. I come back to that damn photo of me and Lamar. This man was really in love with me. If his brother hadn't broken my heart we would still be together, I never had any desire to be with Lamar, I don't know what he thought was going to happen with him springing this house on me. Seeing this picture made me curious as to what else he had of us in here.

I move from room to room, scanning for anything that may lead someone to think that Lamar and I were more that just in-laws. I come to the bedroom and spot a photograph on the nightstand. Getting closer I see it was from Eric's 40th birthday celebration. The image looks odd, picking it up I see Eric has been cut out and the picture staged as though it was just me and Lamar.

This fool was obsessed!

I pick up the frame and continue my hunt. Surveying, I conclude that there is none of my DNA laying around. I can't take the chance of being spotted coming out of the front door, so I go out the back, my car will just have to wait. I sprint out the subdivision, coming out by a bus stop. I was in luck too, because I see a bus drawing near.

Climbing aboard and taking a window seat midway in, I take in everything that just occurred. If I would have approached the suspicious car the first or at least the second time I spotted it, I probably could have avoided some of the things that has transpired today.

The name West was a name I hadn't heard or thought of in years. Adam West was my graduate school love, my first love if I'm being honest. My parents weren't as shocked as I assumed that they would be, introducing them to a white man during one of their visits. Maybe it was because he was so handsome, its hard being mean or rude to a good-looking person. The dark hair, green eyes, and athletic build always seemed to make people treat Adam with the utmost respect.

We met at CU's first party of the year, hitting it off instantly by having a conversation about Architecture; my major. Where most people hated when I talked about buildings and designs, he seemed sincerely interested. Columbia University had one of the most historic and beautifully built structures in the U.S. that I had ever seen. I could be stuck in a trance staring at any given area on campus. Adam was there studying political science, hoping to follow in his father's steps in working for the government in some form or fashion, but the way he was able to discuss with me belvederes and oriels, you would have thought we shared the same major. He later explained to me that his grand-father was in construction and taught him a lot.

We dated for about a month or so before I was comfortable having sex with him. I never told him, but he was my first, I thought we would be together forever. My bubble was soon burst when he had the nerve to sleep with my roommate. He begged and pleaded for my forgiveness, but I dropped him like a bad habit. You had one time to cross me and I was done. I have always been like that, man or woman. Shortly after we broke up though, he jumped from the 4th floor balcony of his apartment. I couldn't bear to continue there in New York, so I transferred to Savannah, completed my studies, received my degree, met Eric soon after, and I moved on with my life.

Frank being here in Atlanta is more than bizarre, he couldn't have been no more 15 when I was with his brother. With all that is going on right now, I don't need him un-scabbing any old wounds. I pull out his number I had stored in my handbag. Now wasn't a good time, but he will definitely be hearing from me. Its because of him that Lamar is gone before his time.

Don't ask me why I shot him; it was just a reaction, that's all that I can tell you. Lamar was starting to work my last nerve, but I needed him around a little longer. I didn't want to, but getting rid of him now, especially with the news I received today and Frank showing up running his damn mouth about some mess he knows nothing about, Lamar being gone was best for me. I didn't need Lamar attempting to play thug police, trying to piece puzzles together.

Athaliah.

I can hear my mother calling me that. If she could see what I've been up to; a knock off Athaliah, the daughter of Ahab, slaughtering those around her to keep control of her situation.

Chapter Thirteen

"Last stop."

The piercing voice of the bus driver brings me out of my daze. I look up and I am all the way in Marietta, outside of the CCT station. I am the only one left on board, except for the misshapen vagrant in the far back, laid across the seats in a deep slumber. As I moved forward toward the door, I notice Stone's Bar and Grill among the nearby facilities. A stiff drink would be nice right about now.

"Excuse me Miss." I hear when I get ready to step down.

Catching the stench before completely turning around, I find sleeping beauty behind me desiring my attention.

"Yes?"

"Could you spare a few dollars so that I can enjoy a hot meal tonight?"

For it is in giving that we may receive.

I can hear my father reciting his favorite quotes from Francis of Assisi. I reach down into my bag to salvage any cash I had inside. I come up with a ten-dollar bill and give it to him.

"You have a good night Sir."

"God bless you my sister."

I take my praise and continue out onto the street, making my way in the direction of Stone's, pulling out my cellphone.

"Hello."

"Hey Viv, It's Kat." Vivian has been a friend , a real friend of mine since I came to Georgia.

"Kat! Hey!" She sounded stunned and excited to hear from me. "What's going on?" She continues.

"Just wanted to know if you would like to join me for a drink, I'm at Stone's on Windy Hill."

"Yeah girl, I'm on my way, see you in 15 minutes."

Chapter Fourteen

Entering, the thick smell of cigarette smoke with a hint of various other odors slap me in my face, briefly throwing my senses out of whack. I make my way to the bar and choose a stool at the furthest end and plop down.

"Whatta have?" The tatted bartender asks me while clearing the area around me of empty glasses and used napkins.

"Whiskey neat, Coca-Cola back." I give my request, throwing my bank card on the counter. "I'll start a tab."

"I'll need your I.D."

I hand her my license to hold until I was ready to cash out.

"Hey. You're the wife of that preacher, sorry for

your loss."

Ugh. Really? Give me a break.

"Thank you." I reply, exhausted from all the bullshit I've been receiving today.

"First round is on the house." She offers, giving me a sentimental smile, tapping my cards down on the bar. I thank her with the warmest smile that I can muster at this moment.

I exhale as I observe the atmosphere. Sports played on all the many flat screens throughout the establishment, patrons played pool in the back corner, and one lonely soul danced on the dance floor.

I can sense eyes on me, my muscles begin to tense. I dart my eyes across the room, locking eyes with someone to my left. Someone unfamiliar.

The light skinned, clean shaven gentlemen was definitely not family to the West's. I have no idea who he is.

He notices me notice him, grins, and begins to walk in my direction. Not in the mood, I spin around in my seat and discover my drink. Grabbing hold of it, I raise it up to the bartender as a sign of appreciation.

"Hey beautiful, you alone?" I am greeted as I take a

sip from my glass.

"No, I'm waiting on someone." I shoot back dryly, evading any additional eye contact.

He gets the picture and strolls off. That's one arena I never had any problems in; getting men to approach me. Getting them to stay faithful was a whole other story, seemed like I was never good enough.

Flee also youthful lusts…

The scripture from 2nd Timothy pops in my head. If only the men who claimed to love me practiced the teaching in the Bible, maybe, just maybe, we wouldn't be here right now.

But when he stands praying, forgive.

I hear my mother's rebuttal in the distance. I pick up my cup, and toss the liquor back. My mother, the righteous Elizabeth Hill always had a bible verse ready, and my father always there backing her up. They lived and breathed the word of God, but I never saw things as clear cut as they did. It wasn't always just black and white. I know the bible inside and out, had to growing up. But when you are hurt or betrayed by someone you love, the last thing you think about is scripture. And when it's your husband who is proselytizing it and doing all the cheating, it makes you question your faith all together.

I reach for my glass that has been refilled and go to sip from it.

"Hey Sis."

Chapter Fifteen

It was good to see Vivian. She was what I called my ratchet friend. She didn't take any mess from anyone; would snap on you in a heartbeat, but could be the sweetest person you ever met. She was a blast to be around.

Vivian was a radiant dark chocolate Amazonian, standing 6 feet'1. She has the most beautiful natural hair with curls that if pulled, would bounce right back into place. Looking at her you wouldn't believe that such a striking woman didn't have a man to go home to. This was quickly understood, when you find out she has three children under the age of five by three different men, drowning in debt, and smoked like a chimney; and I'm not just talking about cigarettes. I could smell the spoor of the marijuana as I embraced her in a hug. The smell made me crave a drag from it, but no one knows I smoke and I want to keep it that way, plus Vivian smoked from a pipe like a teenager.

"Girl you know you smell like a walking blunt, right?"

"Girl bye, this my natural scent now." She replies with a chuckle, brushing me off.

"Thanks for meeting me." I move on.

"You know I'm always available for you girl. What you drinking?" She leans forward to look at the variety of liquor, resting her exposed breast on the bar.

"Whiskey."

"Oh no, I don't do the brown." She states, lifting her hands to get the bartender's attention.

"Let me get a Cosmopolitan please."

"Let's sit at a table." I suggest as she receives her beverage. I lead us to the side where there were a row of booths and slide into the middle one.

"So how you holding up?" Vivian waste no time.

"I'm good."

"Listen you not sitting in here drinking like an old white man because you good."

I skate my glass between my hands across the table,

refusing to admit she was right. I wasn't fine. I had given up my future for Eric's, standing by his side, helping him become one of the most recognizable preachers in the world, knowing that a life in the church wasn't what I had intended for my life. All for him to cheat on me on with a tramp that was married as well. Oh yeah, you didn't know that did you? Yeah, Simone ass is married too, and the kicker is, Eric and Derrick were best friends, been since they were in grade school.

I slept with Lamar as pay back. The sex was some of the best I've ever had though, I can't lie. He unleashed something inside of me that I didn't know was there. Maybe I did and just didn't want to confront that part of me. I could be myself around him. He was just free in who he was, it made me feel like I could be too.

Now they're dead, I have Frank white ass stalking me, and a detective running around asking all kinds of questions. I have no idea who I am anymore.

"Kat, no one expects you to be okay." I forgot Viv was here. "You just lost your husband for Christs sakes. If you don't want to talk about how you're feeling, that's fine. If you just want to drink until we forget our names, I'm okay with that too." She comforts, grabbing my hand, stopping my movements.

"Viv, a detective came to see me today." I blurt out, needing some release.

"A detective, why?"

"He says Eric didn't just die but that he was murdered."

As I speak tears begin to drip from my face without effort. All the shit that has went down tonight, no telling what's the cause of these emotions right now.

"Murdered!" Vivian yells out causing people to look and stare. She catches herself and leans in, practically tilting the table-top.

"Murdered Kat?!" she whispers.

"I know. He was poisoned."

"Kat this is crazy. Are they positive?"

"They seemed pretty sure to me, all in the church this morning asking questions, looking around."

"What?"

"Yep."

"Who would want to kill a Pastor?"

"I gave them Maurice name, caught him in my office, snooping around in the dark."

"Serves him right! Let them interrogate his stupid

ass!" Vivian exclaims. Maurice and Viv dated for about a year when out the blue, he tells her he was tired of playing daddy to her bad kids. Although Maurice was well into his forties, he carried on like an adolescent, but he has always been like an uncle to me, and I felt bad insinuating that he could have possibly had something to do with Eric's death, but his demeanor just wasn't right earlier.

"Vivian, don't say that."

"You're the one that gave the police his name, not me."

"I know but I don't think he would actually murder someone. He has some sneaky ways, he's definitely up to something, but murder; I don't think so."

"Well, who could have done it then?"

I hang my head declining to let the words come out of my mouth.

"Kat, do you know something you're not telling?"

I take a deep breath. "Eric was cheating on me."

"Ooaa I knew it! I knew that nigga was no good. All uptight and shit all the time, and all up in the church trying to lay hands on somebody. When all this time he was nothing but a wolf in sheep's clothing. That why

I can't mess with no religious man, its just not natural being all holy like that. That motherfucker."

She was reacting as though she was the one that was being betrayed, hitting her hands against the table and carrying on.

"My goodness Viv. You want the whole world to know? Chill before you knock over the drinks."

"I'm sorry girl, but why didn't you tell me? How long has this been going on?"

"Far as I know, 6 months."

"Damn, that's fucked up."

I sip from my glass, emptying it. Vivian joins me and scoffs hers down as well. I wave two fingers in the air to get the bartenders attention. She reads my signal and gives me a thumb up to let me know my order is on the way.

"I caught him and Simone in the act." The alcohol was loosening my tongue.

"Simone? Simone, Simone?"

"Yes bitch. Simone!" Brown liquor seemed to shorten my temper every time. I'm already stressed, I just need her to calm down on the dramatics. "Caught that hoe sucking his dick, in our house. In our bed."

I thought the waterworks were over, but the tears return, streaming down my face like a river. I immediately dab them away with a napkin as the waiter comes up. I take the cup from his had before he has the opportunity to sit it down and wolf it down, placing another order before he departs.

"I am so sorry Kat." She grabs my hand again.

"Me too."

"Murdered, huh?"

"Apparently."

"Did you do it?"

Chapter Sixteen

"How could you ask me something like that?"

I know she didn't just ask me that shit. I mean, she really had no filter. I feel my eye lids stretching, expanding, growing bigger than what they were meant to. My blood begins to boil at the blatant disrespect.

"Listen, if my man, let alone my husband was sleeping around on me, I'll cut his penis off first. I'll do it slow too, let the bastard feel the pain. Shit, I don't know what I would do after that, probably slap him in the face with it or something."

I can't tell if she is making it into a joke, trying to lighten my mood or oblivious to my obvious aggravation. Regardless, I feel myself getting drunk and I am not feeling where this conversation is going or her prior comment, that she casually apologized and discounted. I won't say anything though, I had to be careful of my actions moving forward, I don't want to do anything else that I may regret later.

"My bad sis, I didn't mean to upset you." She acts contrite. "But you know we all have a little crazy inside of us, we are all capable of anything when pushed to our limits. I'm not saying you did it, or even capable of something like that, but didn't you move down here because…"

Before she could finish and before I knew it, I had my drink in my hand, throwing it into her face. If I was anyone else she would have jumped up trying to whoop my ass, but instead she wipes the liquid from her eyes and shakes the residue from her fingertips.

I don't stick around. I'll pull my purse over my shoulder and turn to walk off. I am sick and tired of being tried. Every time I turn around, someone is trying to play me like a fool. I've been going along with it, if I'm being honest, but not anymore. I have had enough, and I think I have officially cracked.

"The only reason I ain't stomping your ass right now is because you my girl and I know you going through something right now."

I hear her yell out after me. I was really on my own from this point forward. Maybe that is how it needed to be. Being on my own would allow me to keep my head down, get through this temporary hiccup, and move onward with my life.

Chapter Seventeen

Kathryn is awakened by the loud clanging of the dump trucks coming through her gated community, picking up the week's trash. She had taken an uber home last night, falling face down on the couch and into a deep sleep as soon as she walked in. Waking up groggy but somehow refreshed, she makes her way into the kitchen to make her morning coffee. She tells herself that yesterday has passed and today was a new day.

Now who is this? She asks herself when her cellphone begins to ring. Detouring to where it laid on one of the end tables, she sees that it is her mom. She looks at it for a minute, debating whether she wanted to answer. She assumes her mother has heard the news from the police by now and goes to answer her call, but she is too late, the call is missed. Feeling as though she had dodged a bullet, she exhales. Her relief comes too soon, because the home phone begins to chime.

"Hi mom." She answers on the second ring.

"Katty, how are you doing sweetie."

"Fine." She continues to the task of making her pot of coffee.

"A detective just left here, a Mr. Keith Crane."

"I spoke with him yesterday, he came by the church." A flash of yesterday's events beginning to rush to her memory, she quickly shakes them away.

"So, you know what they're saying? Why didn't you tell me?"

"It has been a lot to take in."

"I know baby. He says they don't have any conclusive suspects at this time, that they won't stop investigating until they have someone in custody, so that is good. They'll find out what happened and who could do something so awful, don't you worry."

"This whole thing is a nightmare." Kathryn utters then falling silent.

"We're going to get through this Katty. I'm worried about you, with all this that's going on. How about I come over and we go grab a bite to eat and maybe clear our minds with a little shopping spree."

Kathryn would usually decline immediately but she considered her mother's proposal. This could be a chance for her to forget about everything and act as though all was normal.

"You know what? That actually sounds like a good idea. Let's do it."

"Okay, I'll be there shortly."

While the coffee brews she runs upstairs to jump in the shower and prepare herself before Elizabeth's arrival.

Chapter Eighteen

Stepping out the shower, Kathryn hears a knock at the door and is immediately spooked, she knew her mom couldn't have made it over that fast, she lived thirty minutes away. She freezes mid-step and listens to see if they will give up and go away. The knock returns, this time heavier and more rapid. Dripping wet, she grabs the towel off the sink and wraps it around her. Pushing her damp hair away from her face, Kathy tiptoes toward the front door.

Coming up to the entrance she leans forward to look through the peephole and spots Detective Crane. She hesitates to answer, but when he knocks on the door again, she swings the door open quickly as though irritated with his persistence.

"Yes?" She lets out. Towel now dampened by the

water falling from her body and head.

Crane is thrown aback at the way she came to the door. It wasn't just the way she opened it but the beauty that exuded from her and he knew for sure now that she really had no clue as to just how gorgeous she was. He took her in, trying to imprint the image into his brain; looking her over, up and down, bringing his eyes back up to meet hers, his mouth agape.

"How can I help you?" She says after he fells to speak.

"Umm. Yes, good morning Mrs. Knight." He is finally able to talk.

"Good morning, what can I do for you?" Kat asks, adjusting her form, putting all her weight on one leg, propping against the door.

"I just wanted to ask you a few more questions, is now a bad time?" He asks, lifting the notepad in his hand pointing out that he notices her in her bath towel, and noticing her irritation.

Kathryn lets out a sigh, "No. It is not a bad time. Come in Detective." She opens the door wider for him to walk through. "Please make yourself at home. If you will give me a minute to get dressed, I'll be right with you."

"No problem. Take your time."

Kathy runs into one of the downstairs guest bedrooms where she kept some of her clothing. Attempting to push the door closed behind her, she fails to close it completely, it remains open slightly.

She drops her covering, baring it all, unaware that the Detective in the next room has the perfect view.

She pulls her hair up into a ponytail and feels his eyes on her. She slyly looks over her shoulder and sees that she has an audience. Kat doesn't let Detective Crane know that she knows he is watching, but continues to dress herself. She had never been ashamed of her body and wasn't about to begin now. And the fact that someone as fine as Detective Crane was looking upon her toned body, gave her more confidence and turned her on in a way that she hadn't anticipated.

His light brown eyes followed her every move as she put on a pair of leggings and an oversized tee-shirt that hung off one shoulder.

"Would you like some coffee?" Kathryn asks, walking out the bedroom, catching the officer discreetly trying to adjust his clothing to hide the growth beneath his pants.

"Coffee would be great, thank you." He responds, standing, following her into the kitchen.

"So, what's new Detective? Any developments?" Kat starts the conversation while pulling two mugs from the cabinet and placing them on the counter.

"Well first let me start by apologizing for your lost, I failed to tell you that yesterday. I stopped by your office again before I left, but you had already gone."

"Thank you. Yes, I couldn't take being there any longer." A wave of melancholy covers her face, she turns her back to him and puts a tablespoon of coffee into the brewer.

"I can understand that." Crane sits down in a chair at the breakfast bar and corrects his position before continuing. "Were you and your husband having any marital problems?" He looks up at her curiously.

"No more than your average married couple. That doesn't change just because he was a pastor and I was first lady." Kathryn turns back around facing the detective with an enthralling grin on her face.

"We had our problems." She finishes, pouring the now made coffee in the mugs in front of her.

"Cream or sugar?" Kathryn asks, pushing the canisters in his directions.

"Thank you." Detective Crane accepts, making his coffee to his liking.

"You mind telling me what some of those problems were?"

Kathryn begins to speak, but stops before she could start. She drops her head, closes her eyes, and covers her face with her hand.

"I'm sorry. I didn't mean to upset you." Keith stands to walk around the island to console her, but she puts her hand up, stopping his advance.

"It's okay. I'm okay. Thank you." She wipes her face and breathes out deeply. She brings the mug to her mouth, taking a sip, she continues. "My husband was cheating on me. That was the only problem we ever had. She glances up and meets the Detective's eyes that displayed concern and pity.

"Follow me outside?" She asks walking toward the French doors that led to the patio.

Not responding but doing as suggested, officer Crane follows Kat outside onto the courtyard, where he parks himself at the table. Kathryn reaches inside the center piece and pulls out a pack of Marlboro Reds and a lighter. Opening the pack, she takes out a cigarette and lights it, throwing the pack down on the table as though she had had enough of the conversation already.

Crane places down his notepad and pen in front of him and straightens his posture. "Can you tell me a little about the affair?"

Kathryn looks at him as though he had lost his mind asking such a question. She blows the smoke from her mouth and into his face, causing him to clear his throat and sit back in his chair.

"I don't know much, just that him and Simone were sleeping together."

"Simone?" She is interrupted.

"Simone Clark. She and her husband are members of the church, have been since we began." Kathryn takes another draw from her cigarette. "I found out a few months ago." She releases the smoke through her nostrils. "You have to understand detective, this is very hard for me."

Crane clears his throat again, waving the smoke from in front of his face. "Understandable. Did knowledge of the affair cause much conflict in the home?"

"What do you think?" She answers irritated, putting her cigarette out and standing. "Are we done? Cause I really don't like where this conversation is going. It's like you are questioning me or something." Putting her hands on her hip.

"Technically I am questioning you." Keith could tell that he had hit a nerve, but she walked herself into that one. He grabs his belongings and stands as well.

"I think you know what I mean."

"I didn't mean to upset you."

"You didn't, huh?"

"No, I did not, and I'm sorry if I did." He walks to her and grabs her hand, holding it delicately. Kathryn felt a jolt as he takes hold of her. Looking into his eyes, she could tell he was feeling something for her that he wasn't supposed to. He exhibited feelings of concern and intimacy.

"I am just doing my job. The line of questioning is routine. Don't you want me to find out who killed your husband, so you can move forward with your life?

With my life, or with you detective? Kathryn thinks to herself.

"Of course, I want you to Detective." She squeezes his hand, then releasing it.

"Okay, can we finish talking?"

"Now is not really a good time, my mother should be here any minute."

"Well, how about coming down to the precinct a little later today?"

"Can you come back here tonight, I don't feel right being in a police station?" She counteroffers.

"I can do that." He responds pleased, tucking his writing pad in his pocket. "Well, I guess we're done here."

"Let me walk you out." She says, walking him to the door to exit.

Opening the front entrance, they are met by Elizabeth. "Well hey guys."

"Hi mom."

"Hi Mrs. Hill." Crane acknowledges her, reaching out his hand to shake. "Good to see you again."

"You too. I know we just seen each other but any news? I'm assuming that's why you're here." She quizzes, stepping into the foyer, causing them to step back.

"Just some follow up questions." He responds, hoping that it wasn't evident that he was attracted to her daughter.

Crane was not one to allow himself to catch feelings for a suspect or any one for that matter, that had anything to do with a case. There was something about Kathryn; however, that caused him to not think clearly. She was in fact a suspect, spouses are always the first suspect in a murder investigation, but he couldn't believe that such a marvelous woman can be capable of such a thing.

He didn't know how to respond when she told him that her husband had cheated on her. The only thing that kept running through his head is, how? Why? He just couldn't believe it. If he had someone as wonderful as Kathryn she would never have to worry about him straying. Keith was raised by a single mother and two oldest sisters. Watching his mother's interactions with suitors and the heartbreak his sisters felt when deceived, there was no way he would do something like that to someone he loved. It was too soon to tell, but he felt like she was the one, like her husband's untimely death, him being assigned to the case, and meeting her, seeing her in such a vulnerable state; it was meant to be.

Although, he felt this way, he still had a job to do, and he would do it efficiently and professionally.

"Oh, okay. I'm sorry to barge in on your investigation. This is just so horrible, I still can't believe it was murder. Is there anything that I can offer that would help?"

"Umm, mom, Detective Crane was just leaving, and we have plans remember?" Kathryn cuts in.

"Yes, I sure was Mrs. Hill." Crane co-signs. "Mrs. Knight, I'll see you a little later." Turning to Kathryn to put in concrete their plans by locking eyes.

"Yep." Kathryn lets him out and closes the door behind him.

"Isn't he adorable?" Beth asks rhetorically as soon as he is out of sight. "He would be perfect for your cousin Dominque, don't you think?"

"Dominque? The stripper?" Kathryn retorts appalled.

"Listen, you're going to learn. You need to remember the story of Rahab, a woman full of sin, but found freedom through the power of God's grace. Her past does not have to dictate her future. A nice detective might do Dominque some good."

"Whatever you say." Kathryn cringed at the thought of Dominque's grimy hands intimately caressing the smooth skin of Keith Crane. The sensation she got when she noticed him watching her get dressed made her nervous and excited about him stopping by later tonight. It was dangerous but maybe he would help her get her mind off things, and she could steer him in any direction she wanted him to go.

"Look, I'm hungry. Where we going to eat?"

Chapter Nineteen

"I would like to report a murder." Frank West walks into Zone 2's police department, stopping the first uniformed officer he sees.

He was black and blue from his encounter with Lamar but determined, he held his head high. The voyage to this moment was a rough one for him, but he whole-heartedly believed that Kathryn Hill had something to do with his brother's death. He met her only once and had gotten an unpleasant feeling from her. His notion was solidified by his attack. The thug that she had assault him was even more proof.

He thought he had been careful in trailing her, but guessed he was wrong. Frank wears his bruises proudly, adding a limp for effect. His plan was to use his face as evidence as he told his theory, hopefully making the police take into consideration his words.

Frank is escorted to a desk where an older woman sat typing intensely.

"Have a seat." He is instructed by the officer he stopped in the hallway.

He does as he is ordered, expecting the lady cop to stop what she was doing and tend to him.

"Excuse me ma'am." He attempts to grab her attention, but only getting acknowledged by her holding up her index finger, giving the message to wait a minute.

She continues to type vigorously until she stops, grabs her mouse, and clicks around a few times. "Okay." She turns to Frank. "I'm officer Parks, how can I help you today?" She clasps her hands together, appearing impatient.

"I need to report a murder. See I know she killed my brother. And then she sends a gangster to beat me up! Look at my face! This woman…"

"Hold on. Slow down." Officer Parks interjects an edgy Frank, lifting a pen and sheet of paper. "Now lets back track, what is your name son?"

"Frank West."

"And your brother was killed?"

"Yes, Adam… Well, it was ruled a suicide, but I know she murdered him."

"Suicide?" Parks throws down her pen and reclines back in her chair. "Now you know Mr. West we have a lot of work to do here, real work?"

"Wait, wait." Frank scoots up. "Hold on, let me explain. It was ruled a suicide but I'm one thousand percent sure that he was murdered."

"Okay, tell me why you believe your brother was murdered?"

"Adam would never kill himself. We had plans the next day, it just didn't make sense, and he was dating this girl; Kathryn, and he didn't want to be with her anymore because she was becoming obsessed. As soon as he allegedly jumps from his apartment window, she leaves the state. If that isn't evidence then I don't know what is."

"It's not. None of what you just said proves murder."

"I wish you would just listen to me!" Frank feels himself getting angry. "Look I have been following this woman, look what she did to my face!"

"So, you're admitting to stalking?"

Frank lets out an exasperated sigh and falls against the back of his seat.

Somewhat feeling sorry for him, Parks decides to throw him a bone. "Alright listen, the most you have here is an assault charge." She picks up her pen, "Now who is the assailant?"

"I don't know who the man was, but I know who was with him; who sent him. The woman who killed my brother."

"Alright, what is this woman's name?"

"Kathryn Hill."

Chapter Twenty

"Kathryn Hill? As in Kathryn Hill-Knight?"

Frank had finally gotten the officers attention. "Yes, yes. That's what I've been trying to tell you, she is a murderer and she had a delinquent do this to me!"

"Mrs. Knight is a pillar of our community and a grieving widow, you can't possibly expect me to believe that she killed someone."

"Is there anyone else in here that can help me?!" Frank stands abruptly and shouts, frustrated. "I'm trying to tell you Kathryn Hill killed my brother and probably her husband!"

"Whoa. What is going on here?" Detective Crane walks up at the tail end of the outburst.

"This woman is not listening to me!" Frank screams, pointing at the lady officer.

"Parks, you mind if I take it from here?"

"Sure. Take him." She responds, both pissed and relieved.

"Follow me." Crane leads Frank to his office, closing the door behind him. "So, what's going on?" He wastes no time in getting to the bottom of things once they are inside.

"Man, I just wanted to report a murder." Frank crosses his arms, fed up.

"Who died? Have a seat."

"I'll stand."

"You're making me nervous, sit down."

Frank reluctantly sits in one of the three chairs that were available.

"Now who was murdered?" Crane asks once he is comfortable.

"My brother Adam."

"And you believe Kathryn Knight killed him?"

"Yes!"

"Okay, calm down. I'm trying to help. What would make you think that?"

"They used to date back when he was in college. He told me that she was starting to get weird, crazy, and that he was going to break up with her. Next thing you know it, he's dead and she's down here in Georgia." Frank unfolds his arms and adjusts himself in his seat.

"Mrs. Knight had to be in college over ten years ago and she's been married for 9, why say something now?"

This was the furthest Frank had ever gotten with anyone when trying to talk about his assumption. "I tried to tell them. I tried to tell everyone. I knew that Adam could never kill himself, he loved his life, but I was young, and no one wanted to listen. They ruled his death and suicide and Kathryn got away with murder. I tried to confront her last night and she had her male friend do this to my face." He ends his speech by pointing his finger at his face.

"Looks pretty nasty." Crane admits, acknowledging his wounds.

"Yeah, I'm surprised he didn't shoot me. He held that gun right up to my head, I was sure I was done for."

"Do you know what kind of gun it was?"

"Black, that's all I know."

"Did you get a look at the male? Can you describe him?"

"He was African-American, at least six feet, 180lbs, I guess. I couldn't really see since I was getting beat into a bloody pulp."

"Any witnesses?" Crane had begun to write everything down.

"Besides Kathryn, there was the worker at the Exxon off 285 East, exit 25. He heard all the commotion and came outside to see what was happening, causing them to flee."

Still taking notes, Crane finds it peculiar that Kathryn would be accused of murder around the same time her husband's death was ruled one.

"Are you getting all of this?" Frank asks, lifting and hovering over the detective's desk.

"Yes, I am. Did you see the car?"

"Yeah, a silver Mercedes."

"Happen to get a license plate number?"

"FLZ-2393."

"Okay, I think that's all the information I need." Crane states, clicking his pen, placing it down, and standing.

"Wait, that's it?"

"For now, yes. I will look into the allegations of

murder and assault."

"Then what?"

"Listen Frank, let me do my job. I promise I will investigate this to the fullest extent of the law. Your claims have to be proven, I just can't just go around arresting people just because you say so."

"I understand." Frank wanted more but he felt hopeful. He extends his hand to be shaken. "Thank you, sir. Will you keep me posted?"

"Absolutely, leave your information up front and here is my card if you think if anything else."

Chapter Twenty-One

Kathryn was surprised that she had such a good time with her mother. They had enjoyed in laughter, had good food at the Avenue, and did some great shopping at Atlantic Station. She wondered why it couldn't be like that all the time. Today was the longest she could ever stand being around her. Kathryn enjoyed herself so much, she hadn't thought once about all the things that have been going on. But now she was home and couldn't help but to.

As she sat at the dining room table, a wave of loneliness comes over her. Dropping her head into her palms, she couldn't think of one person that she could call.

Rubbing her eyes, smearing her make-up, she pours another herself a glass of vodka on ice. I am becoming an alcoholic. She thinks to herself. Taking in a mouthful there is a ring at the door. Staggering to the door, she goes to open it. As their eyes meet neither one can bring their mouths to open. Kathryn attempts to slam the door shut but is stopped by a foot.

"Go away! Why are you here?!" She yells out, hit to the floor by the forceful push of the door.

"You know why I'm here you bitch!" Frank steps over Kathryn, making his way into her home. He thought about waiting for the detective to investigate but, assumed he would be brushed off and pushed aside like so many times before.

She pulls herself up from the floor, her glass still in her hands, never spilling a drop. Frank ignores her dismay and marches around the ground level, taking a look into every room, seeing if they were alone.

"What do you want?" She asks.

"Just to talk to you." He responds, taking a seat on the sofa and crossing his legs.

"Want something to drink?" Kathryn offers as she swallows from hers. Dismissing him and his apprehensions.

She doesn't wait for him to answer, she walks into

the kitchen to retrieve another glass then proceeds into the dining room where the bottle of Tito's was sitting on the table.

"Ice?" She rhetorically asks, making her way to the freezer, plummeting two ice cubes into the cup.

"Here." She holds the crystal in his face.

Frank sits there staring at her as though not sure how to react. He has vaguely remembered what Kathryn looked like but seeing her now, he couldn't deny her beauty, it was almost overwhelming. He feels himself relaxing as her eyes burn into him. He takes the glass from her hands and brings it up to his lips, letting the liquid fall down his throat and landing in his stomach where it smoldered like a fire; he rests against the couch, thinking the liquor may give him some courage.

Kathryn sits in the arm chair next to him. "Why are you here Frank, after all these years? I'm not saying its not good to see you, its just a little strange."

Frank takes another swig before he speaks, collecting his thoughts. At ease now, he didn't want this to turn nasty if it didn't have to. "Well." He begins, taking another sip, feeling his nerves take over. "It's about Adam."

"What about Adam?"

"I don't believe he committed suicide."

Kathryn waits for him to elaborate.

"It just wasn't like Adam. Kathryn, if I'm being completely honest, I believe you know more than you are telling, more than you have ever told."

"Frank, I loved your brother more than life itself. Although he broke my heart, his death was hard on me too. You never know what's going on in someone's mind."

Frank gulps his drink and reaches to place the empty container down on the coffee table. "Ohh." Dizziness takes over his sight, the room begins to spin, and the glass misses the table and crashes to the floor, breaking into several shards. He grabs his head, trying to stabilize his vision.

"That's the thing about the mind, it contains secrets. And the thing about secrets Frank, is that they are supposed to stay that way." Kathryn continues, stepping closer to Frank, placing her hand on top of his head.

"What did you do to me?" He slurs, struggling to

get up.

"Just relax." She pushes him back against the cushion.

Frank eyes begin to roll, and he realizes Kathryn had put something in his drink. "You drugged me." He states, feeling himself losing control.

"Rohypnol." She runs her fingers through his hair. "You never should have come here Frank."

Frank, no longer being able to keep the inevitable sleep at bay, closes his eyes and drifts off. Kathryn picks up his arm and lets it fall lifelessly back down. Sure, that he was inoperative, she begins to clean up the mess from the spilled alcohol. With the liquid cleaned from the floor and the broken glass swept and thrown in the trash, she returns to where Frank laid unconscious and sprawled out on the sofa and picks him up from his arms, pulling him down onto the marble, dragging him to the basement.

Frank was a very scrawny fellow, but his lifeless body was heavy and difficult for Kathryn to maneuver. She grunted and grumbled as she made her way through the halls. Finally arriving at the basement entry, she opens it and pushes Frank down the stairs, watching as he tumbled down, hitting the bottom with a thump. She comes down behind him and checks his pulse to see if he was still breathing.

"You just had to come fucking with me, didn't you Mr. West?" She talks to him, realizing he was still alive. "Your white ass should have known better." Kathryn antagonizes.

Lugging him to a dusty chair, she throws him into it, using up all her strength. She bends over, putting her hands on her knees, catching her breath. Noticing Eric's work area, she goes over and takes away a roll of duct tape and rope. Kathryn begins to tie Frank to the chair, yanking his arms around the back, tying together his hands. She ties his feet to the legs of the chair, and tears off a piece of duct tape, securing his mouth to keep him from being able to speak once he comes to. She looks at him wondering what she would do with him next.

SLAP!

She couldn't resist slapping him across his sleeping face as she thinks of the audacity he had, thinking he could just pop up and interrupt her life. It was because of him that Lamar was dead in her eyes, and now look what she was forced to do. She goes to slap him again when she hears a rustling upstairs. Quickly shutting off the lights, she runs up the flight of stairs.

"Crane?" Kathryn pulls the basement door closed behind her as she reacts to Detective Crane's presence in her house. "What are you doing?" She asks, seeing that he had his gun drawn.

"Your door was open. When there was no answer, my first instinct is danger. Are you alright?" He places his gun back into his holster.

"I'm fine. I had no idea the door was open. Do you think someone is in here?"

"I don't know, but I got a good look around down here, want me to look around the rest of the house?" Crane offers going into protection mode.

"Would you please?" Kathryn bats her eyes, reeling the detective in, wrapping her arm inside of his as they begin to walk up the staircase to the second floor.

Crane lets go of her the moment they reached the top, releasing his gun from its resting place and holding it high before moving forward into the study.

"Stay out here." He demands.

Finding no one inside, he returns, and they make

their way into every room, before ultimately arriving at the master bedroom. Crane slowly pushes open the door and creeps inside, Kathryn close behind him. Looking in the walk-in closet and then the bathroom, he come back out into the room, catching Kathryn picking up some of her delicates that laid sparingly around the room.

"Excuse the mess, last thing I expected was for someone being up here."

"You should see my place. I definitely have you beat in the mess department." Crane jokes, putting his gun away. "Looks like no one is here."

"Thank you, Detective."

"Call me Keith."

Kathryn looks up at him at the informality; surprised. "Keith, thank you." She rephrases with a grin on her face.

Her smile sends chills through Crane and the fact that he was in her bedroom suddenly becomes uncomfortably clear. "Want to go back downstairs and talk for a sec?"

"Here is fine." Kathryn drops on her California king. "Come." She says, patting the area beside her.

"Uh, that wouldn't be appropriate, Mrs. Knight. Get up."

"Oh, come on Keith, call me Kat. Sit down, let's talk." She replies seductively.

A hesitant Crane loosens his tie while trying to read her. *What is she up to?* He asks himself. Wanting to find out, he sits down next to her as requested.

"Now, what would you like to talk about?" She asks, scooting back against the headboard and releasing her hair from its ponytail.

Crane watches her hair falls softly around her face. He had come there on a mission; to investigate her husband's death and to gets some answers to some new developing questions that came from his unexpected conversation with Frank West. His duty was on its way out the window, as his flesh was taking over. He was so attracted to this woman that he didn't know what to do. There was no way he was going to be able to do his job effectively if he was going to be in her presence.

"Detective?" Kathryn lets the words crawl off her tongue, slow and low, as though whispering a moan into his ear. She licks her lips and places a hand on top of Crane's.

Crane quickly slides his hand out from under hers and tries to gain his wits about him. "Your husband. Umm, I want to talk to you about your husband."

"What about him?" Kathryn jerks back.

"When we spoke earlier, you were telling me he was having an affair."

"Yeah, so?"

"I looked into Simone and her husband and they both have an alibi. It checks out."

"And Maurice?"

"Maurice, may be stealing from the church, which is a motive for murder, we're still considering him as a suspect."

Tears that seem to fall like the rain as of late begin to fall from her eyes and she drops her head. Keith moves closer to her, placing a hand on one of her legs that were crossed Indian style. Her eyes still closed, Kathryn snatches him up and embraces him in a hug, burying her head in his neck.

"My heart hurts." She weeps into him. "It hurts so bad." She tightens her grip, adjusting her position, climbing into his lap as though an infant getting rocked to sleep.

Crane rubs her back, taking the opportunity to smell her hair, that smelled of lavender and coconut. "I'm sorry this is happening." He soothes.

Kathryn lifts her head at his words, their faces so close their noses slightly touch. "I feel so safe with you." She lightly kisses his lips. Forgetting himself, Crane closes his eyes and falls into the moment.

"Will you protect me?" She kisses him again, this time lingering. She turns her body in his lap, straddling her legs around him, facing him completely. Wrapping her arounds around his nape, she feels his manhood pressing against the inside of her thigh.

"Will you Detective?" Kathryn asks again, licking his closed lips as if they were covered with whipped cream.

"Yes." Crane lets out in a moan, picking her up in his arms and flipping her around onto the bed then mounting her.

Hovering over her he gazes into her eyes; eyes that were vacant and indecipherable. She grabs his face and pulls him in for an intimate exchange of tongues. Fully immersed, Crane pulls his lips away to plant them on her neck; kissing, biting, and licking from her neck to her shoulder, traveling down to her chest. Removing her shirt, he devours her nipples one at a time, delivering licks with a fast flick of his tongue. Kathryn brings his head back up so that she can kiss his lips once more, tugging at his button up, attempting to take it off. Crane assists in the process, revealing eight pack abs on a hairless abdomen.

Kathryn glides her hands from his chest down to his navel, lifting to lay kisses on him. Both ready for the next phase they remove their respective bottoms. She bites her lip at the sight of Crane's dick, that had to be nine to ten inches at least.

"Put it inside of me." She insists, anxious.

Crane had condoms in his wallet but didn't want to mention it. Looking at her pussy; bare and wet, he wanted to feel every bit of it. He falls on top of her and gently slides himself into her.

"Mmm." They wail in unison.

Grabbing her ass, Crane passionately kisses her and they fall into the perfect rhythm.

"You feel so good." The words escape Kathryn.

Crane strokes deeper and he feels his legs begin to shake. "What's that?" Crane stops his movements abruptly, hearing a noise.

"I didn't hear anything." Kathryn tries to bring him back to her, throwing her pelvic up, grinding against him.

"No, wait." Crane pulls himself away and listens for the sound again. "It's my phone." The humming noise that he heard was his cell phone vibrating in his pant pocket.

"Can't it wait?" Kathryn was horny and wanted her relief.

"No, I'm still on duty." He reaches into his pants and takes out his iPhone. "Crane speaking." He answers. His body instantly stiffens. "I'll be there in twenty." He ends the call. "I have to go." Crane states to Kathryn, putting on his clothes.

"Why? What happened?"

"There's a body."

Chapter Twenty-Two

Crane

The Lieutenant couldn't have called at a worse time. I have been waiting to get up in that first lady since I met her. I could tell she wasn't uptight like most women that are into the church. There was something in her eyes that let me know she liked to get down. The fact that she let me slide up in her raw may be a red flag, but the shit felt damn good.

The call came at a good time too, cause the white kid showing up at the station couldn't be a coincidence. His brother's death and Pastor Eric dying seemed to be all tied together with one common denominator; Kathryn. If she did have anything do with them, I don't need to be getting caught up smashing a suspect. The girl is so fine and seems so innocent, I want to help her in any way that I can, but I also made a vow to enforce justice and I must put my badge before anything else, even if it causes blue balls.

I pull up to a brick house where police cars, forensics, and the coroner were all parked outside.

"What do we have?" I ask a uniform getting out of my car and walking under the crime scene tape.

"Black male, mid-thirties, gunshot wound to the head." I am brought up to speed.

Walking inside the home, I get a whiff of the decomposing corpse. "Has he been identified?" I ask lieutenant Lopez as I approach, covering my nose.

"Working on that now." I am answered by a CSI instead of my superior.

"Time of death?" I probe, pulling a pair of latex gloves from my back pocket, and moving toward the body.

"Twenty-four to forty-eight hours. It's hard to tell by the decomp, and the heat in here doesn't help things; the thermostat was set to 89 degrees. Full autopsy will need to be done to be sure."

"Now who would have the heat on that high when its already over 90 degrees outside?" I ask myself but speaking aloud. I take in the scene; the position of the body and the gun, and something isn't adding up.

"Lieutenant." I say, standing and taking off my gloves. "Lieutenant, this appears to be a suicide, why am I here?"

"I'll tell your why." He shoos off the officers that were standing around him, and waits until they are all gone before continuing. "Guess who that car outside belongs to?"

"I don't know, who?" I inquiry, hands on my hips.

"Kathryn Knight."

Now I can't think of one reason why her car would be outside this house that had a dead body inside of it, but the shit is getting way too weird. The fact that I was just knee deep in her pussy less that twenty minutes ago leaves me speechless, and I start to smell her on me. I feel myself looking stupid as I try to think of something to say.

"Why do you think her car would be here Crane?" The Lieutenant doesn't wait for me to respond and rattles off another question.

"I don't know, sir."

"I'll tell you why. She had something to do with it, that's your answer." He shakes his finger in my face. "Johns told me he overheard you talking to a young man earlier today who was shouting around that Kathryn Knight killed his brother. Is this true?"

"Yes sir, I am looking into it. Frank West brother's death was ruled a suicide ten years ago, back in New York. I wanted to have more information before bringing it to you, could be nothing, could be he is just still grieving. I…"

"Sir, you have to see this." I am interrupted. "We have identified the body."

Lieutenant Lopez and I walk over to the screen that displayed the findings from the fingerprints.

Lamar Knight.

It was Lamar Knight laying over there on the sofa. "Damn." The words flee from my mouth.

"You damn right damn. What are the chances that brothers die within a week from each other Crane?" The lieutenant was getting fired up. Eric Knight's case was very high profile, everyone was looking to see how this thing would unfold. Lopez was under a lot of pressure from all the media attention. Finding the killer and closing the case was top priority.

"It looks like Lamar's wounds are self-inflicted." I try to reason.

"And Eric just died of sudden hear failure! No Crane, Kathryn Knight's car being here is a sign, she knows something; she's a part of this mess." Lopez begins to pace, scratching his balding head.

I scratch mine too. This shit was crazy. Could Kathryn really be capable of something like this? If you could see her you wouldn't think so. She is perfect; her lips, her smile, those eyes, and that body. It's not just sex appeal, she's so fragile and meek, I'm not buying it.

"Found something." We hear an officer call out from down the hall. He was calling out from a linen closet. "Take a look at this." He says as we draw closer.

We come up to the closet entry and see what looks to be a shrine to Kathryn. Newspaper clippings, pictures, candles, and a television.

"It gets better." One of the officers say, inserting a VHS into the t.v. Once the tape is in, the video begins to play automatically and it is a sex tape. Lamar and Kathryn Knight going at it in what looks to be a laundry room.

"That's it!" The Lieutenant says aloud. "Sampson, Jones, get in touch with Judge Paulson and see if we can get a search warrant for the Knight Estate. Simpson, Montego, go sit outside her house and wait for it to come through." He delegates.

"Sir, think about it. So what if Kathryn was having an affair with Lamar. He was obviously obsessed with her, look at this. What if he killed his brother to be with her and the guilt ate at him, so he took his own life?" Hell, that sounded plausible to me.

"We are dealing with a black widow here Crane!" The Lieutenant turns away from me to finish giving orders.

"Please, just let me go over and speak with her. I have gained a rapport and I think it'll be easier to get information out of her than sending police cars to sit outside her home would. My goodness, her husband just died sir."

"And she killed him Crane! Are you serious?! Simpson, Montego, go!"

"Lieutenant, we don't know that she killed her husband, I think she'll be more forthcoming if I speak with her first, trust me on this."

Lopez weighs what I just said, and I can tell he is thinking about it hard, as he rubs his hand across his chin. "Okay, if you believe that you can pull something out of her, go, but I'm sending an unmarked car over as well."

Chapter Twenty-Three

Kathryn lays on the bed, naked and aroused. She almost had Detective Crane where she wanted him. She knew her world was crumbling around her, and that having him on her side was the most important thing at this point. Unable to reflect in a way that she needed to due to the pressure between her legs, she grabs a pillow from her bed and sticks it between her thighs and squeezes until she climaxes, releasing the tension from her clitoris.

Kathryn elects to attend to her captive down in the basement. She puts back on her clothes and makes her way to where he sat tied up and gagged. Opening the basement door, she hears Frank rustling around below. Gliding down the stairs, taking two at a time and hoping he couldn't free himself, she spots him.

"Well, well, well, look like we have ourselves a little escape artist." Frank had gotten one hand loose and was working on the other, but he freezes at the sight of her. "What do you think you are doing?" Kathryn asks, yanking his arm back around the chair, tightening the rope.

"Ouch!" Frank winces at the pain from the twine digging into his skin.

Kathryn picks up the tape that had been ripped from his mouth and thrown on the floor, and goes to replace it.

"What do you plan to do?" He spits out quickly before she has the chance to cover his mouth again.

Kathryn smirks at him and pulls over a crate and sits on it, bringing it close to him. "What were your plans in coming here?" She counters.

"To prove you are a murderer. I found out you spent some time in Porter House right after moving here; you were institutionalized." Frank speaks matter-of-factly.

"I was grieving!"

"Or you had a psychotic break. I guess it didn't help, seeing that you just murdered your husband too. Can't help yourself, can you?" He continues to taunt her.

"You don't know what you're talking about, just shut up! Shut up!" Kathryn squawks angrily, slapping the tape back on his face, muzzling his speech.

"Arghh!" She stands and screams, knocking over the crate she was just sitting on.

Truth is, she has no idea what she is going to do about Frank. She knew that she couldn't kill him, not in her house; there was no way she would be able to dispose of the body.

How did he find out about Porter House? Those records are supposed to be sealed. She talks to herself.

Kathryn paces the basement floor, running her fingers through her hair, trying to think of a solution to her predicament. She hadn't thought about her stint at Porter House in years. She had spent about six months there after moving down here. Admitting herself in, she told her parents that she was doing a mission in Haiti with an old school-mate. If it was in the name of the Lord, Mr. and Mrs. Hill didn't ask any questions. But Kathryn knew something wasn't right inside, that she had a dark side, especially when it came to matters of the heart. She couldn't stand it; how men thought they could play with it without a care in the world and expect you to be okay.

They have to pay. She encourages herself.

Where did he park? Who knows he's here? The thoughts hit her suddenly, and she races back upstairs and looks out the living room window. The only car she knows is the one that was following her, and she didn't see that one out there. A sigh of reprieve discharges from her body, and she allows herself to fall down on the chaise that sat under the windowsill.

As soon as her form eases, the doorbell rings. Frank must have heard it as well, because Kathryn could hear him begin to moan and stomp loudly. She runs over to the entertainment system and turns on the stereo and let the loud vocals of Whitney Houston drawn out his groans for rescue. As Whitney sings how she will always love you, Kathryn goes to the door and answers it at the second ring.

"Back so soon?"

Chapter Twenty-Four

Crane refuses to look into Kathryn's eyes, in fear that he may not be able to keep up his strength to do his job. He walks past her, leaving her confused. She closes the door behind him. "What's the matter?" She asks concerned.

Crane turns around to face her. "Lamar Knight is dead."

"What?!" Kathryn shrieks bringing her hand to her mouth, covering it; exhibiting surprise.

"Can you tell me why your car was parked outside the crime scene?" The detective grills, trying to read her.

"Well." Kathryn begins, walking back over to the chaise. "I don't know. I let him borrow my car. He came to the church stating that he needed to run a few errands and if I minded him driving my car for a while. I said no of course, and that it." Kathryn had plans on sneaking over and getting her car that night once the Detective had gone.

"Then how have you been getting around?"

"I haven't, I've been here, except when I went out with my mom." Kathryn shoots back. "What is this about Keith?"

"Stop. Call me detective." Crane brushes her off, not believing anything she says at this point. On the ride over, he replayed everything that has occurred since her husband's death. She was hiding something and trying to distract him with her beauty.

"You weren't saying that about an hour ago, Detective." Kathryn picked up on his vibe, folding her arms across her chest.

"Listen, I'm not even going to lie to you, you are a suspect in your husband's murder and now in Lamar's."

"You have to be kidding me?!"

"I'm not, so tell me about your relationship with your brother-in-law."

"What?" That question was the last thing Kathryn expected. "Why would you ask me that? He was family."

"Was he more than that?" Crane moves closer to her, and he could feel her heart beating outside her chest.

"Stop! I don't like these questions, you're sick!"

"The photos in the home indicate that you were more than in laws."

Damn. Kathryn says to herself, she thought she had been thorough.

"I mean he had a little thing for me, but it was never reciprocated."

"There's a sex tape Kathryn." Crane alerts nonchalantly.

"Tape?! What tape?!" She shouts, dumbfounded.

"Look, none of this is looking good for you."

Kathryn could tell that Crane was there strictly as a cop, she feels the walls closing in on her. Tears begin to swell in her eyes and a lump appears out of nowhere in her throat. She starts to weep loudly which causes Cranes guard to lower. He resists the urge to swoop her into his arms and hold her tight.

"Why does everyone around me always die?" She cries harder, and Crane can no longer hold it in, he goes to her and wraps his arms around her, allowing her to sob on his shoulder. He is a sucker for her tears.

"What if the person that killed Eric, is coming for me next? Maybe Lamar knew they were coming for him and that's why he killed himself." Kathryn lifts her head up from Crane's chest and speaks through snivels.

Detective Crane pushes her away from him. "I never said anything about Lamar killing himself. What would make you think that he did?"

"Well didn't he? I could have sworn you just said that." Kathryn tears dry up and her mind swims.

"No, I didn't."

Kathryn steps away from him and walks over to the fireplace. "I believe you said it. In fact, I'm sure you did."

Crane looks at her behavior and realizes that the Lieutenant was right. As her back is turned to him, he pulls out his phone and sends a text to Simpson and Montego, who were outside and alerted them to call for backup. He swiftly places the device back into his pocket as Kathryn turns back around toward him.

"Want something to drink Detective?" She asks detached.

"No, I have some more questions." Crane responds walking to turn off the music.

"Well, I need a drink." Kathryn starts toward the kitchen.

"What was that?" He wanted to know when he hears a loud crash that echoed throughout the house. Crane pulls out his gun and inches forward.

Kathryn becomes immobilized at the sound and what that meant.

"HELP! HELP! I'm down here!"

Chapter Twenty-Five

Crane moves towards the sound of the cries with his gun in tow.

"Wait!" Kathryn yelps, attempting and failing at obstructing his path.

Crane pushes her to the side with a callous look in his eyes. "Police! Where are you?" He speaks out.

"I'm done here! Help me!" Frank hollers.

"Where do you think you're going?" Crane says to Kathryn who is tip-toeing to the front door. "Come here." He grabs her by the arm, drawing her to him, hauling her with him as he continues to the door where he was sure the voice was coming from. He sprints down the staircase and into the cellar with Kathryn in one hand and his weapon in the other.

"Frank West?" Crane is stunned at the sight of

Frank tipped over onto the floor, tied, and a piece of tape loosely hanging from his mouth.

"Detective Crane." Frank is relieved to see a familiar face.

Crane slings Kathryn into a corner as he kneels to release Frank from his restraints. He pulls him up and looks to Kathryn for answers. "Explain!" He demands, but receives nothing from her.

"I'll tell you! I came to confront her about Adam and she drugs me and throws me down here. I told you she was crazy!" Frank roars, lunging toward Kathryn to attack but is stopped by Crane.

"Is what he is saying true Kathryn?" Crane redirects his attention back to her.

"He broke into my house." She retorts in a low and defeated tone.

"I did no such thing!" Frank launches at her again, this time almost landing his open fist on her face before Crane was able to get to him.

"Why didn't you just call the police if that was the case Kathryn? This doesn't look good at all." Crane asks, disappointed at the events that were unfolding. He was not envisaging this when he came over.

Kathryn refuses to speak another word, leaving Crane no other chose but to approach her with handcuffs. "Kathryn Knight, you are under arrest. Turn around." He reaches to grab her shoulder to forcefully turn her when she throws back her elbow, bashing him in his nose, then snatching his gun from his possession.

Crane falls back onto the ground, holding his nose that is now bloody. Frank picks him up and supports him until he is stable.

"You think that I'm going to let you arrest me?" Kathryn yells, pointing the gun at them.

"Whoa." Crane throws up his hands. "Calm down, we can talk about this."

"Talk about what?! Huh?!" She waves the pistol at him. "Talk about how I'm tired of no good ass motherfuckers messing around on me?! Wanna talk abut that? About how his white ass brother having to nerve to cheat on me with my roommate while I was asleep in the next room?!" Kathryn focuses the gun on Frank and pulls the trigger, hitting him in the thigh.

"Ahhh!" Frank collapses in pain, shrieking out in agony.

Crane moves for Kathryn but is quickly met with the barrel of the gun aimed at his head.

"Let's talk Detective. Let's talk about my husband, the Lord's prophet, who I gave up my life for. I wasn't meant to be a first lady, I did that for him! Let's talk about how I came home and caught him in bed with another woman! And Lamar. Lamar fucked everything up. No, wait a minute." She turns the gun back to Frank. "It was this bitch! He fucked up everything, had Lamar asking questions that he had no business asking." Kathryn becomes enraged and fires another shot, this time hitting Frank in his other leg.

Frank passes out at the shock and Crane falls beside him to check his pulse.

"And you Detective. I almost had you." Kathryn strolls over to him and rests the firearm to the middle of his forehead. "It could have been something nice." She bends down and kisses his lips then stands, cocking the trigger to shoot and end this nightmare.

"Freeze! Put the weapon down!"

Chapter Twenty-Six

The courtroom is completely still. The only noise you hear comes from the low whispers of the spectators and the flash of the many media cameras that are in attendance. This story of love, betrayal and murder is the biggest story that this city has seen since the Wayne Williams case back in '82.

Kathryn Hill is from a small town outside of Atlanta, Georgia. She is the only child to Lucas and Elizabeth Hill. Elizabeth is an elementary school teacher and Lucas works at the local mill.

The Hill parents were your typical middle-class All-American black family. There was plenty of love throughout the house, and they attended church every Sunday at His Glory Baptist Church were Mr. Hill was assistant Pastor.

They weren't rich by any means, but Beth and Luke made sure their little Kathy had everything that she needed, and tried their very best to see that she received the things that she wanted as well.

For the life of them they couldn't understand what occurred between her birth thirty-five years ago and now, that would lead them into this courtroom where they are hoping and praying that the Lord will have mercy and that the jury will not find their baby girl guilty of murder.

Where did they go wrong?

The Hills can barely recognize their daughter, who once radiated a light so bright, you could see her coming from a mile away. The disheveled, worry ridden shadow, with bags as big as coin purses under her eyes, was just a shell of the once beautiful woman so many knew and respected.

Dreading and anxious of the return of the jury, Kathryn sat so low in her chair that you would have thought she was only a head and a pair of legs.

"All rise." The bailiff cuts the air with his loud and commanding voice. The congregation all cease in making sound. It was as though everyone had stopped breathing; you could hear a pin drop.

The bailiff proceeds to announcing the returning presence of the judge presiding over the case.

"Please send in the jury." Judge Greg Paulson instructs the bailiff.

Opening the door, all twelve jurors walk in one by one and take their seat.

"Have you reached a verdict." The judge asks.

The foreperson of the group, an overweight tense looking woman rises from her seat, "Yes your honor, we have."

"On the first grounds of First-Degree Murder, how do you find?

Nervous Susie looks over to the defendant, to the judge, and in her shaky palms, she looks down at the sheet that contains Kathryn's fate.

Clearing her throat, "On the first grounds of First-Degree Murder, we the jury find the defendant guilty."

The entire room gasps, finally catching their breath just to lose it again.

"On the ground of Second-Degree Murder, how do you find?"

"Guilty your honor."

Wails from Elizabeth rock the room and vibrates the walls. Her husband grabs her, pulling her to him and burying her into his bosom. At the distraught image of Kathy's mom, the reporters have a field day and the camera bulbs start to flash so fast and bright it blinded many that surrounded the family.

"Order! Order in the court!" Judge Paulson bangs his gavel demanding silence. "And Madam foreperson, on the grounds of Attempted Murder, how do you find?"

"Your honor, on the grounds of Attempted Murder, we find the defendant, Kathryn Hill-Knight... Guilty."

The crowd is in an immediate uproar. Some filled with joy, many in awe, and few filled with sadness.

"Order! Order!" The gavel strikes down again. "We will reconvene in one week from today for sentencing. Court Adjourned."

Kathy stands from her seat, looks over to her devastated parents, tears streaming from her face for the very first time since the trail began.

The bailiff comes, grabbing her arm, preparing her for the handcuffs, he turns her back towards him. At the click and clack of the metal, Kathryn faints, dropping to the floor, and everything goes quiet.

Epilogue

It was my first year of grad school when I met Adam. I didn't usually go for the guys outside my race, but this white boy had some swagger about him. He had an aura about him and you knew he was going to go places in his life. Standing 6'5, Adam was tall, dark hair, and had the most alluring crystal blue eyes. When he asked me out, I thought it was a joke, so I turned him down. I knew we had great conversation when we did talk, but actually trying for a relationship, I wasn't feeling it. He was persistent, he continued to ask me out until I gave in and said yes.

I fell in love instantly; as soon as he kissed me I knew. We would grow old together, have kids, and take over the world.

The day that I found out he was screwing Thresa;

my roommate, behind my back, it's like I snapped. I didn't understand, and when confronted he laughed at me, said that I was an experiment, that he just wanted to see what it was like to sleep with a black girl. My whole world was shaken.

I showed up at his apartment one day just to talk. He was drunk when he answered. He came at me as though our argument never happened. He began to try to kiss me, telling me he loved me, that I was the prettiest thing he had ever seen.

"Then why cheat on me?" I had asked. He had put his finger on my lip, telling me to hush, tugging at my clothes. I was disgusted, the total disregard of my feelings. I push him away. "You know you want it." He says to me, throwing me onto the bed and getting on top of me.

"Stop Adam. Get off me!" I yelled, but he kept on, holding me down with one hand and unbuttoning his pants with the other. I knew what was about to happen and I couldn't believe it. I cried for him to stop but it was like he couldn't hear me. As I try to push him away, he strikes me across my face. Everything that I've ever known goes away and I believe that's the day my I turned to stone. I grab the lamp on the nightstand and whack him across the head with it. He stops fighting me and becomes still as blood gushes from the side of his skull. He falls down on me and I quickly push him off.

I knew that I couldn't leave him there. The sound of the subway outside made me realize that the window was open. Adam's apartment was on the fourth floor, the fall would finish what I started. I was saving women all over the world who had the potential to get hurt by him. I pull him from the bed and hold him up to the window and with a slight push, he goes over and to his ultimate death.

I thought my stay at Porter House cured me, stop the bad thoughts, and strengthened my mind. I was wrong. Seeing Eric fucking that whore took me back to a place that I never wanted to go back to. Yeah, it was me, I killed him. I sure did. I had been lacing his drinks and food with arsenic for months, from the day he came home like everything was gravy; like he wasn't just stinking up our bedroom four hours before. I guess that Sunday was the kicker. I wasn't intending for him to collapse in front of the congregation but I'm glad that he did, shows them that cheating never pays.

Maybe I messed up, maybe I've paved the way for women following me, or maybe I have showed men that nothing good comes out breaking a woman's heart.

All evil began with the woman; Eve. But it doesn't have to end with the woman.

I can hear my mother's voice vibrating off these concrete walls. Still, I can't escape her.

My, how far the fruit has fallen.

~

About The Author

Born and raised in Atlanta, Ga, African-American novelist Krys King found her passion for Romance while reading books by bestselling authors like Terry McMillan, Omar Tyree, and E. Lynn Harris. Krys began her writing with poetry, even getting some published nationally during her childhood and winning Editor's Choice Award for the simply named poem "*You.*"

The married mom of two burst onto the Atlanta literary scene in 2017 with her bestselling sexually-charged modern romance *Crossed in Love*, a story that seduces you with sex, love, friendship, and betrayal; causing media outlets from all over to know what drew her to write such a powerful love story and what readers should expect next. The proud self- published author founded The LuvvSyc Alliance the following year, wanting to make the self-publishing process for her fellow writers easier.

Although adding businesswoman to her title, Krys King is still writing and looking to publish what he readers have been dying for next Spring; sequel to *Crossed in Love – Consequences of Love*.

"I just want to tell entertaining but relate-able stories about women and love and how you can't have one without the other and how you can't know one without knowing the other."

-Krys King

Helping Writers
Become Authors

theluvvsycalliance.com